I0737993

# THE PLAGUE

## THE SOCIALIST PESTILENCE

John L Bowman

The cover is an image of a plague doctor, a physician who treated victims of the bubonic plague or Black Death. Their mask was bird-like with a beak to protect them from being infected by the deadly disease. They believed the disease was airborne, so the beak was packed with sweet smells such as dried flowers, herbs and spices, which they believed would prevent transmission.

(Source: Pixabay, https://pixabay.com/images/search/plague%20doctor/)

# CONTENTS

# Preface

The Plague is a book about socialism. It is a redacted and condensed version of my book *Socialism in America*, which William F. Buckley, Jr. wrote was *a very good rundown on all the weaknesses of socialism.* For simplicity, all references and the bibliography have been removed, all quotation marks removed and quotations from sources italicized (including the back cover copy), all sources are credited in the text, and some quotes have been modified. Some sources are listed at the end of this book.

# Introduction

The political philosophy of socialism is becoming more acceptable for many Americans. This is a mistake, and this book is about why.

Princeton professor Friedrich A. Hayek wrote about his firsthand experience with socialism in Germany during the 1920s and 1930s and the consequences. He warned of the parallels between socialistic thinking in America during the 1940s and the German socialist thinking of that period. One of his warnings was that socialism in Germany was brought on mostly by *people of good will, men who were admired and held up as models in democratic countries.* It was these people who championed greater freedom, justice and posterity but unwittingly brought on socialism and eventually National Socialism (Nazism). Their cherished ideals produced results utterly different from those expected. He describes these people as becoming horrified as National Socialism progressed, horrified with the realization that their cherished beliefs had led them directly into an abhorrent tyranny. Many who had supported the movement to National Socialism in Germany *stopped supporting it at some point in its development and were forced to leave their country.* Professor Hayek's words should catch your attention.

Some Americans have come to embrace socialism because they are disenchanted with capitalism. Some are tired of being poor and struggling with debt; they think some people do nothing and get everything, that the economic system is rigged against them and that the rich are living off the poor. Others think capitalism makes people selfish and corporations greedy, which leads to disparity of wealth. Many others think they have a right to food, housing, education and health care—it should be free. And a few just want to get things for free without working.

Let me ask you socialist sympathizers, if American capitalism is so bad, why does everybody want to come here? Why is America inundated with illegal immigrants? Why do the caravans of people from Central America wind their way north to America and not south to socialist Venezuela? Why do communist Cubans risk their lives to cross ninety miles of water to get to America? Indeed, one sign in a window in Havana read "where is Lee Harvey Oswald when you need him." And why do so many wish to escape socialism and communism worldwide? Why did communistic East Berliners risk their lives to reach capitalistic West Berlin, and why did the Chinese in communist Kowloon seek to reach capitalistic Hong Kong? And why is it that many of the founders and advocates of socialism preferred to live in mercantile countries?

Saint-Simon, Fourier, Owen and Blanc all lived in non-socialistic countries, Karl Marx lived in capitalist England, George Bernard Shaw preferred England and André Gide, an ardent communist, returned home and renounced communism after visiting the Soviet Union. The truth is many people who live in socialist and communist states want to leave.

This book is written to those Americans who are wavering in their belief of the American dream and contemplating socialism. It will endeavor to persuade them that socialism is not part of that dream but a political system that will end it. This book will explain why socialism is wrong for them and rebut those pro-socialist, anti-capitalist reasons mentioned earlier for wanting it. This topic will be expanded on at the end of the book in a section called The Vision.

I should mention that even though I personally despise socialism, I have grudgingly come to the belief that a minimum amount of it is necessary for any civilized society. Everyone needs clean water, roads, sewers, police, food, basic education and some health care. My principle concern and target of this book is when socialism is taken to excess, particularly with its parent: communism. I should mention that I admit capitalism also has flaws, but I believe capitalism with its vices is far preferable to socialism with its virtues.

This book first defines socialism, briefly describes its history and founders, gives a short history of socialism in America and then presents arguments against it. The arguments are grouped under those that relate to the individual and those that relate to society. The book ends with a vision for America.

# *Part I*
## Defining Socialism

Socialism is the state owning and controlling the means of production and distribution of wealth on the basis of "from each his ability, to each his need" — it is a collectivistic philosophy. "From each his ability" refers to the production side, where everyone shall work the best that they can, and "to each his need" refers to the distribution side, where everyone's basic material needs shall be guaranteed. Socialism is collective because in order to function it requires the able to provide from ability. It must suppress individualism, unlike capitalism, which encourages and rewards it.

Using this definition, many policies and philosophies that implement the socialist program can be identified as truly socialistic. These include redistribution of income, excessive regulation of business, nationalization of industry, a planned economy, guaranteed "cradle-to-grave" benefits, a minimum wage, Medicare, Social Security and universal health care. These truly are socialistic because they involve the state control of production and the distribution of wealth based on need.

# *Chapter One*

## History of Socialism

Socialism has passed through three broad phases: the utopian phase, the violent phase and the Fabian phase. This chapter will describe some of the principle socialists of each phase and their ideas.

The word socialism first appeared in English in 1839 as an adaptation of the French word socialisme, which was coined seven years earlier. It is interesting to note that almost all of the early socialistic thinkers were French, which gives rise to the observation that socialism is essentially French in origin. Socialism's rise is most often attributed to the rise of the industrial society and the consequent development of the working and urban classes. In reality, it may have been due to the French peasants, who had a long simmering resentment against the oppressive French monarchy.

The movement began in the early 1800s in France with Saint-Simon and the Utopian socialistic thinkers.

# Utopian Phase

The first one hundred years of socialism is considered the utopian period. It was during this time socialist thinkers such as Saint-Simon, Fourier, Owen, Proudhon and Blanc dreamed of a better world where poverty and misery would be eliminated. It is called utopian because their utopian ideas were imaginary and generally unworkable. Robert Owen could be considered an exception because he was an industrialist who actually instigated certain socialistic policies within his capitalist business.

## Henri de Saint-Simon (1760-1825)

Saint-Simon, a French aristocrat, is considered the father of socialism due to the publication of his book *On Social Organization* in 1825. He approached his conception of *new ideas and forces* from an economic viewpoint focusing on the producer. His method was intended to promote their welfare by experts directing and improving the means of production. He broke with historic thought by proposing that the population be given priority in state expenditure, ensuring work for all men so that they *may secure their physical existence.*

## François Charles Marie Fourier (1772-1837)

Fourier's goal was to obtain a social order that would secure perfect happiness for all people. He proposed phalansteries, or collective labor associations with co-proprietorship and profit sharing. These phalansteries would be analogous to the great hotels of Switzerland where all the comforts of life could be found. Private property was not to be abolished, and rich and poor were to be intermingled. Everyone would receive a share of the phalanstery in proportion to the amount of capital they were able to put in, which would gradually transform naturally into common shareholder property. Each phalanstery would guarantee each member food, lodging, clothing and amusements without conditions. A few phalansteries were organized in Europe between 1840 and 1850, and forty-one were organized in the United States, among which Brook Farm is best known.

## Robert Owen (1771-1858)

Owen was an English industrialist who improved his workers conditions in his New Landmark cotton mill in England. He is considered the father of British socialism.

He established shops where labor could get supplies at cost, instituted strict sanitary rules, built decent housing, restricted drinking, established kindergartens, created a general education system and continued to pay full wages when the mill had to close due to market conditions.

Owen wrote *Social System* in which he championed communism and opposed private property. He proposed the formation of villages of *unity and cooperation* for the unemployed. Eager to put his communistic ideas into practice, Owen purchased thirty thousand acres of land in Indiana for a commune and called it New Harmony. His experiment failed after three years of struggle, and Owen lost most of his money.

## Pierre-Joseph Proudhon (1809-1865)

Proudhon was more anarchist than socialist because he wanted to negate both government and private property. He is most remembered for his belief that private property is theft. He believed that a free society should not be based on the accumulation and circulation of capital but rather on labor or the actual work performed.

## Louis Blanc (1811-1882)

Blanc was a French teacher and politician perhaps best known as the source of the famous socialist phrase *from each according to his ability, to each according to his needs*. He was the first utopian socialist to use the political machinery of his own time to put his socialistic ideas into operation.

His philosophy was simple: the goal of social effort was human happiness. He thought that in order to create happiness there must be opportunity for all. Everyone would be guaranteed work through the erection of social workshops by the state through which the principle of workers' control would be established.

Blanc's famous quote came from his belief that God gave one ability *as a measure of obligation to society*, which he derived from the gospel, which says *whosoever will be chief among you let him be your servant*. Put another way, he believed *the more a man can, the more he ought*. Blanc was the first to shift the focus from the elimination of oppression to the imposition of obligation.

It is edifying to note that Blanc's famous quote violates Hume's law: *don't make an ought from an is* — to give according to need (the ought) does not follow from having ability (the is). For Hume, Blanc is expressing a sentiment and not a moral.

## Violent Phase

The utopian phase failed along with its communes, so some socialists like Karl Marx, Friedrich Engels and Nikolai Lenin started to bring socialism about by force.

### Karl Marx (1818-1883)

Marx is perhaps the best known socialist and is the spiritual leader and prime moving force for socialism in the world today. With his *Communist Manifesto* published in 1847, Marx, along with Engels, abandoned utopian socialistic philosophies and advocated violent, revolutionary class warfare. This line of socialism was taken to extremes by Lenin and eventually became communism in Russia during World War I.

Marx was both a brilliant, albeit sophistic, philosopher and an odious man. He wrote of a harmonious state where the proletariat rules and the state withers away. He also postulated the famous theory of dialectical materialism that he borrowed from Hegel.

In his *Communist Manifesto* he described the rise and development of two great antagonistic classes: the bourgeoisie, the class of capitalists, owners of the means of production and employers, and the proletariat, or wage earners. He postulated a victorious and democratic revolution that centralizes all production into the hands of the state. Once this is done, all property is abolished, a heavy progressive income tax is instituted, all rights to inheritance are eliminated, a national bank is created and all communication and transportation is centralized.

In his book *Capital* he predicted that capitalism would eventually destroy itself because it increasingly exploited the workers who would violently revolt and become the controllers of society. The result would be the elimination of capitalism and private property. Marx is famous for coining many of the commonly used socialistic phrases today including *the workers have no country, the proletarians have nothing to lose but their chains* and *workers of all countries unite.*

In his book *Intellectuals*, Paul Johnson describes Marx as argumentative, violent, alcoholic, shouting, furious, raging, without manners, prideful, contemptuous, dirty, fierce, pessimistic, anti-Semitic, malicious, ignoble, full of hatred, bitter, angry, adulterous and disloyal. He describes the young man Marx as bohemian and idle, lying on the sofa all day, up all night, unwilling to work at a regular job and without self-discipline. He describes him as a man who had a taste for violence, an appetite for power and a tendency to exploit others. He was a hypocrite because he championed the oppressed but denied his daughters an education because they were women. He was a man who conceived an illegitimate son that he never acknowledged or supported. He was also a man who advocated the state provide for the poor according to their needs but never personally paid taxes.

Johnson perhaps grasps the essence of Marx, and socialism itself, when he discusses Marx's motivations. Marx was unwilling to work at a job, borrowed money to live and was incompetent with personal finances, all of which led to life-long money problems and his subsequent hatred of money, moneylenders, usury and capitalists. He was a spendthrift who spent most of his life living off inheritance or loans from family and friends, which he never seriously attempted to repay. Consequently, he was always in debt and unable to support his family, which is why they lived in poverty. He, for example, had a house cleaner he never paid.

Perhaps most damaging of all is Johnson's critique of Marx's philosophy. He wrote Marx's work was a result of his personality and not reason. Marx wrote of finance and industry but knew few businessmen and never visited a factory. He avoided peasants and mixed only with middle class intellectuals. Most damaging of all is Johnson's assertion that Marx often used facts that were wrong, misleading or downright deceptive. Johnson calls *Capital a work that is structurally dishonest, fundamentally flawed, and written by a man who did not understand capitalism*. In short, his work cannot be trusted.

### Friedrich Engels (1820-1895)

Engels, who was an intellectual collaborator and supporter of Marx and the co-founder of Marxism, was an industrialist. He co-authored the *Communist Manifesto* and helped develop the notion of dialectical materialism.

## Nikolai Lenin (1870-1924)

Lenin was a fierce Marxist follower who brought social-ism to its logical extreme by bringing about communism in Russia. He was a hardheaded, ultra-practical, revolution-ary tactician who led the Russian Bolshevik Revolution to become that country's first socialist dictator. He believed communism would eventually envelop the world. He also, like Marx, insisted that this evolution must come about by violent revolution.

Lenin completely rejected the role of a democratic sys-tem of government and its parliamentary system. Instead, he called for a monolithic governmental organization of dedi-cated professional revolutionaries devoted exclusively to dictatorship by the proletariat.

Near the end of World War I, Russian military defeats and worsening economic conditions culminated in the 1917 Russian revolution, which precipitated Nicholas II's abdication and the abolition of the monarchy. The German government was convinced that Lenin, if he could come to power, would withdraw Russia from the war, so they provided him with a special railroad car that transported him back to Russia on April 3, 1917. Some have compared this transport of Lenin to Russia to the act of injecting a healthy body with a pathogen, the train being the needle. The rest is history; the revolution succeeded in bringing the communists to power, eventually making Lenin the dictator of Russia. Lenin lived only seven more years until his death on January 21, 1924.

Marx and Lenin's philosophy is wrong in so many ways it is hard to know where to start. The socialist dictatorship does not disappear but only continues to dictate, the state never withers away but rather becomes bigger and more totalitarian under communism, people continue to not only struggle but also to survive the communist system, the proletariat is not freed from the capitalist but is rather repressed by the communists along with everyone else and any democratic parliamentarism is silenced. It also turns out wealth disappears because nobody works according to their ability when needs are automatically met.

The violent phase of the socialistic history tree ultimately failed with the collapse of the Soviet Union in 1991 and contemporary Fabian socialism emerged.


## Fabian Phase


It became clear to many socialistic thinkers, mostly British, that neither the utopian nor the radical Marxist forms of socialism would work. Consequently, they borrowed the best from both movements and embarked on a new process of socialism called Fabianism. Fabianism is the effort to bring socialistic change about gradually and peacefully, primarily through the democratic process. This is the main form of socialism today and is often referred to as creeping socialism.

The Fabian socialists envision the emancipation of land and capital from individual and class ownership, its gradual transfer to the state and the *gradual nationalization or municipalization of industry*. They consider private property immoral and say that it must be discarded, and they bitterly attack individualism.

It is with the Fabians and their view toward democracy that the first ominous signs of the unique relationship between democracy and socialism began. They saw democracy as their vehicle to achieve socialism — they believe *the economic side of the democratic ideal is, in fact, socialism itself.*

Today socialism is instituted gradually through furtive, unrecognizable and sometimes underhanded means. The socialistic goals of state control over the means of production and redistribution of wealth were recast by the Fabians into attacks on the individual, the vilification of private property, the devaluation of competition and attacks on business and corporations.

A few contemporary Fabian socialists include André Gide and Michael Harrington.

### André Gide (1869-1951)

Gide was a French philosopher, part-time communist and passionate artist. His motivations for socialism were essentially aesthetic. His ultimate aim was the emancipation of humankind from all artificial limitations and the cultivation of all the riches inherent in humanity. He envisioned a communist *new man* that represented a more evolved type of human being.

Gide is a particularly interesting socialist because after loudly championing communism he visited the USSR in 1936 and came away disillusioned. He saw firsthand the true nature and consequences of communism, which were totalitarianism, oppression, poverty and a *gray norm* society with no *new men.* He realized he had been cherishing grandiose illusions mostly of his own making and renounced communism.

Some have postulated that Gide's new man was most likely his way of trying to overcome the societal stigma of his homosexuality. His true motivation may have been to escape the guilt, shame and the judgment of others.

## Michael Harrington (1928-1989)

Harrington is a modern American socialist of the most scary and dangerous kind. Like most Fabian socialists, he believed in using democracy to bring about socialism so the government can allocate resources to satisfy people's needs.

In 1968 he published *Toward a Democratic Left* in which he advocated a more socialistic centralized American government and a new *democratic left* because *the American system does not work anymore.* Because people are economically incompetent and local governments tend to be conservative, he believed all economic planning should be centralized in Washington, D.C., which should impose its own priorities and usurp many local government functions.

Harrington is that very dangerous kind of rabid, inflexible, and totalitarian intellectual socialist described by Paul Johnson in his book *Intellectuals* and Professor F. A. Hayek in *The Road to Serfdom.* Harrington is so ideologically driven he is willing to do anything to achieve his view of utopia like Lenin, Stalin and 2020 Democratic presidential candidate Bernie Sanders. Once power is achieved these kinds of ideologically driven political leaders often become despots and brutally repress people who do not agree with them. Harrington is the Joseph McCarthy of the left and reason enough to oppose socialism.

# Chapter Two

## Socialism in America

It is the Fabian form of socialism that we see in America today, which has advanced indecipherably over the last hundred years and corrupted our Founding Fathers' intentions. Let us first describe America's political origins and then the people who have brought socialism.

### The Founding Fathers and Their Intentions

America's political foundations were in response to English domination, the monarchy and aristocracy. As such, it can be argued that its core revolutionary principles were individual liberty and wariness of centralized, powerful government.

Thomas Jefferson, the author of the Declaration of Independence, opponent of Federalism, third president of the United States and core spiritual father of America, championed individual freedom. He believed in small government and personal liberation. He was highly suspicious of centralized power. He advocated elimination of the federal debt and reduction in taxes. He envisioned a society with minimal government and echoed Thomas Paine's sentiment that the *government is best that governs least*. He wanted a government that followed a *noiseless course unattractive of notice*. He believed that occasional rebellions, such as Shay's Tax Rebellion, were healthy because they kept the government from trammeling individual rights. He thought a *little resistance to government* was good. He resisted the kind of big, intrusive and collectivistic government socialists have brought today.

Kathrin Bowers in her book *Miracle in Philadelphia* described the Founding Fathers' debate at the Constitutional Convention in September 1787 and America's political origin's best. On freedom, Rufus King argued that too much legislation is a vice — he wanted freedom (having just gained it from England). On property the group was not interested in the redistribution of property; rather they were concerned the many poor in democracy would rob from the rich. They believed that property was a right that government should defend. All believed citizens should be allowed to keep self-earned property. Stephen Hopkins from Rhode Island said those who have no property can have no freedom, John Adams said property was a right of mankind as surely as liberty and his cousin Samuel Adams spoke of the right of property.

It is evident that America was founded on Jeffersonian freedom, limited government, individualism and the right to keep property.

Americans believed in these ideals. Future Americans like Ralph Waldo Emerson wrote of self-reliance. American lore is full of the rugged individual, rags-to-riches and a can-do attitude. Before the New Deal, Americans largely did not rely on the government for support; they relied on themselves. This has all changed with the advent of socialism. Socialism is corrupting the Founding Fathers' intentions and ideals.

Socialism's appearance in American society is a relatively recent occurrence. Before 1900 it simply did not exist. If one had to pick a time it infected America it would probably be when Karl Marx moved his First International to New York in 1872. It was this party and its offspring that was the intellectual driving force behind the progressive movement beginning at the turn of the century that influenced Theodore Roosevelt. After that the two early primary catalysts for the rise of socialism in America were the passage of the Sixteenth Amendment to the Constitution in 1913 and the Great Depression of the 1930s.

The Constitution provided that that *no Capitation, or other direct Tax, shall be laid unless in Proportion to the Census or Enumeration.* A capitation tax is a direct and uniform tax imposed on each head or person and is often called a poll tax. In other words, Congress may not levy a head tax or poll tax unless all persons are taxed the same. The Constitution effectively prohibited an income tax because incomes vary; the tax would not be the same for everyone.

This changed in 1913 with the adoption of the Sixteenth Amendment to the Constitution, advocated by democratic President Woodrow Wilson, which authorized a federal income tax . It states that *the Congress shall have the power to lay and collect taxes on incomes, from whatever source derived, without apportionment among the several States, and without regard to any census or enumeration*. With this it opened Pandora's Box, making federal taxation a political tool for social engineering, allowing the federal government to rapaciously grow in size and power and paving the way for the progressive income tax. It also opened the door for the socialists in America and provided them with the tool they needed to institute their policy of wealth redistribution.

The Great Depression gave the socialists, which now included much of the Democratic Party, the second opportunity to institute national socialistic programs. Roosevelt's New Deal was intended to end the depression but did not—it only opened the door wider for socialism. Indeed, the depression returned in the late 1930s and ended during World War II, but the government programs remained.

There have been many pro-socialists in America but the principle instigators of American socialism have been Theodore Roosevelt, Franklin D. Roosevelt, Lyndon Johnson, Barack Obama and the Democratic Party.

# Theodore Roosevelt and Progressivism

Theodore Roosevelt, the twenty-fifth president of the United States, took office in 1901 amid what is called the Progressive Era. Roosevelt himself was initially no socialist. In fact, he was critical of socialists, but ironically his policies commenced the introduction of socialism to America.

Some of his early progressive policies increased the size of government, championed "social justice" and promoted the public welfare, which brought more governmental control. Roosevelt's New Nationalism advocated bigger government and graduated income taxes. His increasing socialistic bent eventually culminated in his New Nationalism, a philosophy that admonished progressives to give up their Jeffersonian prejudices against big government and use the power of government to achieve socialistic ends. It specifically advocated a graduated income tax, inheritance taxes and workers' compensation for injuries or illness. It was his handpicked successor for the presidency, William Taft, who supported the Sixteenth Amendment to the Constitution, which authorized the federal income tax.

Theodore Roosevelt's Square Deal was the forerunner to Franklin D. Roosevelt's New Deal, both of which have become the raw deal for many Americans today.

# Franklin D. Roosevelt and the New Deal

Franklin D. Roosevelt could be called the father of American socialism. Many of his motivations were socialistic. He said, for example, that the Revenue Act of 1935 was necessary to *save our system, the capitalistic system* because it would save the nation from revolutionary turmoil by creating a more *equal distribution of wealth.* With this intention he began the process of transforming America into a socialist state.

His Social Security Act of 1935 is the socialistic mother of them all. It was created to provide security for the aged, indigent, handicapped, and unemployed. It contained three major provisions: pension funds for retired people over sixty-five and their survivors; federal-state unemployment insurance programs; and federal grants for state public assistance programs for the aged, dependent children, the blind, the welfare of children and public health services. The Social Security Act, more than any other New Deal program, committed the national government to a broad, long-range social welfare agenda. It, more than any other program, is the genesis of American socialism. Roosevelt's Revenue Act of 1935 was intended to soak the rich to pay for these programs to the poor; indeed, it was popularly known as the Soak-the-Rich Tax.

The New Deal left in its wake bigger government, increasingly higher governmental spending, higher taxes, progressive taxes, socialistic redistribution of wealth policies, a more planned economy, higher government debt, less free enterprise and more socialism. It laid the foundation for a welfare state and the idea that the federal government was responsible for insuring a *minimum level of well-being for all Americans.*

## Lyndon Johnson and the Great Society

Johnson described himself as a Roosevelt New Dealer. He pushed an array of new socialistic legislation through Congress to implement his new program called the Great Society. It intended it to *declare unconditional war on poverty in America*. His social program passed 435 bills through Congress, including Medicare for the aged and Medicaid for the indigent, which dramatically increased the size and spending of the federal government.

## Barack Obama and the Affordable Care Act

Obama was the forty-fourth president of the United States who contentiously pushed through Congress the Affordable Healthcare Act, derisively called Obamacare. His act required citizens to carry health insurance or face a penalty, required employers to provide health insurance or pay a surtax, taxed higher incomes to pay for the healthcare and prohibited insurers from charging different rates for patients with different medical histories, which essentially vitiated the intention of insurance.

Obama's socialism shifted the cost of healthcare to some in order to pay for all and like his socialistic Democratic predecessors further extended the coercive power of government.

# Democratic Party

Clearly, the Democratic Party of America has been the primary vehicle for the advent of socialism in America. It has instigated, promoted, championed and succored socialism mostly under its cherished mantra of progressivism.

Patching together some of the party's past platforms, the similarities between various words, phrases, programs, ideas and proposals of socialism become obvious, albeit in a deceiving way. For collectivism they say *national community — acting through government — can make a big difference* and *Social Security is more than a government program, it is a solemn compact between the generations*. The terms *national community* and *solemn compact between the generations* replace collectivism.

Instead of directly stating the government should control the means of production, the Democrats state *the private sector acting through government can make a big difference* and champion the need to *stiffen penalties for employer interference with the right to organize,* the need to *enforce worker rights* and the need for a new law *banning permanent striker replacement workers*. They gloat over having *won the battle for increasing the minimum wage* and *defeating a national right-to-work law* and claim they *will protect our wage and hour laws, including the forty-hour workweek and overtime requirements*. They pass legislation that is inimical to the interests of business and production and then jejunely say *we must ensure no tax provision has the effect of encouraging corporations to locate in other countries*. Every one of these platform statements is against business and extends the government's control over the means of production.

They often never state directly a belief in the redistribution of wealth but propose innumerable programs that accomplish the same end. The platform drips with socialism's "from each his ability" when it objects to *tax giveaways for the well-off and well-connected* and complains that *the rich were getting richer, and the poor were getting poorer.*

The most obvious connection between the Democrats and socialism is in their unabated demands that each be taken care of according to need. The concept of "to each his need" is replaced with words and phrases like *security, safety net, the system's protective safety net* and one of their favorite contemporary admonitions to *not leave anyone behind.* They demand *secure Social Security and Medicare for future generations* and a *fundamental guarantee of retirement security.*

One big government Democratic platform claims that *we must continue to decentralize our government* and that *the days of big government are over.* On the contrary, their platforms are imbued with spending programs that necessarily increase the size of government. Statements demand the *increase in after-school care for America's children,* the need to *put one million new well-trained teachers in our classrooms, public support for the arts, including the National Endowment for the Arts and the National Endowment for the Humanities* and that the *federal government defray the expenses of educating children with special needs.* Furthermore the platform supports *Child Health Insurance Programs to help states provide health coverage* and that *the government provision of universal health coverage for all Americans.* Clearly, the Democrats would increase the size of government, increase spending and increase the national debt.

One of the symptoms of socialism is totalitarianism, a label Democrats do not want. However, they exclaim that when any *states do not make progress in improving student performance, the federal government should redirect money from state bureaucrats and transfer it directly to schools that need it.*

The entire Democratic platform is imbued with the socialist philosophy. As the old proverb says, a carpenter is known by his chips. The Democratic platform is collectivistic, it advocates the government control of production and redistribution of wealth and it mandates "from each his ability, to each his need." It is a socialistic platform that will inevitably lead America to the ultimate consequences of socialism, which are loss of freedom, injustice and totalitarianism.

Democrats know the only way to achieve these ideological goals is through the coercive power of government, so their platforms ooze the philosophy of big government directing and providing for all. Everything flows from the government, which controls, forces, directs, manipulates and arbitrates. Thomas Jefferson, who believed in small and invisible government, maximum individual freedom and the unequal distribution of wealth would recoil at this socialistic ideology. Indeed, he wrote (paraphrased) that wise and frugal government shall leave citizens free to regulate their own pursuits of industry and improvement, and shall not take from the mouth of labor the bread it has earned.

It is no surprise that the Democratic Party member-
ship primarily includes the beneficiaries of socialism: single
mothers demanding state-supported child care, the poor demanding state-supported services, the aged demanding old
age security, the ill insisting on state-supported medical care
and government employees whose livelihoods depend on
big, socialistic government. Only the people who provide the
government with the resources to help these groups are left
out of the Democratic platform's equations.

## Bernie Sanders

To one degree or another most Democrats are socialists,
and Sanders, senator from Vermont and popular candidate
for president of United States in 2020, is one extreme example.
He is an avowed socialist who envisions a controlling, directing and manipulating central government enforcing socialist
philosophy. He hates what he calls right-wing ideology and
capitalism and lauds Castro's communistic Cuba because it
brought free education and medical care, even though Castro
killed and incarcerated thousands of citizens.

Bernie is much like Michael Harrington described
earlier with his rabid, inflexible and totalitarian socialistic
philosophy, his desire for a more coercive centralized government to bring it about and the use of democracy to do so
to satisfy need.

Sanders has many extreme leftist positions; his admir-
ing followers affectionately call him Bernie because he is
a socialist promising them a Christmas list of benefits. He
promises to increase the minimum wage, expand parental

leave and vacation time, institute universal healthcare, abolish all student loans and make college free. They also love Bernie because he hates capitalism. He states that wealth inequality is evil, the economy is rigged to make the poor work for the rich and corporations are not paying their fair share. He tells them these programs will be paid for by taxes on the wealthy billionaires, because nobody should earn more than millions, and corporations, with a tax-on-stock scheme. He tells them the rich buy elections and the media is controlled by corporations, and they believe him.

Naturally being on the far left he opposes charter schools and the death penalty and favors LGBT rights and same-sex marriage. Ironic on many levels is his opposition to open borders, which he tells his followers is desired by the far right rich and corporations because they need low-wage workers when it is the left sanctuary cities protecting illegal immigrants and a "far right" rich Republican president Trump in 2020 working to stop illegal immigration. His solution is for American taxpayers to fund poor nations so they don't immigrate to America!

Some claim Bernie is not a socialist but rather a "welfairist" because he wants to model America on Scandinavian countries' socialism and offer extensive benefits to all. Bernie himself says he is a democratic socialist who wants broad-based progressive taxes to pay for extensive social benefits. Make no mistake, Sanders is a through-and-through socialist, and although he may not be a Marxist one believing in class warfare, he certainly incites it. Claiming he is a democratic socialist only evades the appellation—he is just saying he believes in socialism brought by the people.

Whatever he calls himself, Bernie is a hardcore socialist. Socialism is the state control of the means of production and distribution of wealth in accordance with "from each his ability, to each his need." Bernie's political views fit this definition perfectly. Advocating massive regulations and taxes on business and government and control of the utilities and banks in his home state of Vermont is the state control of production. His demand for high progressive taxes and the redistribution of wealth is the state controlling the distribution of wealth. His advocacy for broader progressive taxes also reflects according to ability, and as a welfarist using it to provide extensive social benefits is "to each his need." Bernie ardently denies he wants to model socialism after Venezuela or Cuba but rather socialist Denmark or Sweden (to which Danish Prime Minister Lars Lokke Rasmussen told him Denmark is a market economy and not socialist), but everything he says and does points to the former.

What is really scary about Bernie is that he acts like Marx and looks like Lenin. Marx has been described as argumentative, violent, shouting, furious, raging, fierce, bitter and angry with small, fierce and vicious eyes. Like Lenin he is small and wry, and he has an ardent and inflexible ideologue seemingly willing to do whatever it takes to bring about socialism. Bertrand Russell, who once met Lenin, wrote that he despised the populace and was an intellectual aristocrat—he wrote if he had met Lenin not knowing who he was he would have thought him an opinionated professor. George Orwell, who also met him, believed he was capable of great injustice and cruelty. Could ardent Bernie be the same?

Earlier it was mentioned that near the end of World War I the German government provided Lenin with a special railroad car that transported him back to Russia on April 3, 1917, which some have compared to injecting a healthy body with a pathogen. Could it be the Democratic Party is bringing the likes of a socialist pathogen plague Bernie to America today?

Now let's move on and consider the reasons why socialism is a pernicious political philosophy.

# *Part II*

# The Arguments Against Socialism

There are reasons why socialism repeatedly fails, and there are reasons behind the tocsin of those who have experienced it. This section is intended to expose the reasons for those alarms as well as socialism's chimerical nature, its procrustean methods, its paladins and ultimately its many mean and destructive ways. This chapter will endeavor to expose the emperor so that he may be seen fully without his clothes.

Socialism's destructive nature is presented in two parts. The first are those beliefs and their consequences that relate to the individual, and second are those that relate to society.

# Chapter Three

## Arguments that Relate to the Individual

The first set of arguments against socialism relate to the individual. Each of these arguments is summarized as follows.

### Freedom

Humans wants to be free—people have the right to be free, or, as Thomas Jefferson put it, the inalienable right to liberty. Individuals should be free to act and believe in such a way that does not harm others. Socialism reduces individual freedom while socialism's extreme, communism, virtually eliminates it. The very essence of socialism requires individuals to sacrifice their freedoms to the collective group. The state control of the means of production and distribution of wealth reduces freedom because it requires a controlling, administering entity.

Socialism limits every one of the essential characteristics of freedom. It limits choice, oppresses, steals the fruits of success, owns the individual, limits potential, limits success and failure, diminishes expression, mutes dissent, is unjust and dispenses oppressive and limiting obligations. Socialism is not about freedom; it is about oppression.

F. A. Hayek in his book *The Constitution of Liberty* emphasized the importance of freedom, the importance of tolerance and how utopian socialism diminishes both.

For Hayek, liberty is that condition of men in which coercion of some by others is reduced as much as possible in society. A state in which man is not subject to coercion by the arbitrary will of another or others. It is the *independence [from] the arbitrary will of another*. Liberty does not mean all good things or the absence of evil for Hayek because it is possible to be free and miserable.

Hayek describes how socialists confuse liberty with power. They think liberty means the physical ability to do what one wants, or the power to satisfy one's wishes. This is not liberty but power. It is a bastardization of the very concept of freedom by changing its definition from the absence of restraint and obstacles to the realization of desires. Indeed, some socialists like John Dewey have said that the demand for liberty is the demand for power.

**Historically**

A historic intellectual struggle has been waged for freedom — freedom from oppressive ideologies. The emancipation from church and religion are probably the best examples of this form of struggle against oppression.

G. W. F. Hegel in his *Philosophy of History* aimed to trace the unfolding of freedom in history. He wrote that *the history of the world is none other than the progress of the consciousness of freedom.* Hegel went on to say that genuinely free people do not allow their most important decisions to be determined by oracles; rather they make their own decisions. The modern day oracles Hegel is referring to are the socialist utopian thinkers who believe they know what is best for everyone else. They become the makers of law, the arbiters of freedom and the social engineers of society.

Hegel also thought that universal suffrage would not bring freedom because people would vote in accordance with their material interests. People in a democracy with universal suffrage, according to Hegel, would not vote based on what is just or right but rather on what benefits them. This is what we see today in America under socialism's influence. The captured socialist majority votes for more benefits and in the process tyrannizes the minority by requiring it to pay for the benefits with higher tax rates than those of the majority itself.

Human history has been a long, hard struggle for freedom, and socialism is just another in a long line of oppressive forces threatening that freedom. Socialism represents a return to limited individual freedom and therefore is a recidivist philosophy. It is a relic of the past.

It stands opposed to the human spirit's historic march toward freedom.

This discussion of the human spirit's struggle for freedom is important because it makes conspicuous the relative importance of the ideal of freedom in relation to other ideals.

**Ordering of Ideals**

We develop our ideals from many sources like our beliefs and experiences. Because people have many different beliefs and experiences, they often develop or emphasize different ideals. To complicate matters, ideals often conflict, so if our objective is agreement regarding socialism, the solution would be to prioritize ideals. Three ideals that influence people's thinking on socialism illustrate this. These ideals are freedom, justice and equality.

These ideals often conflict. For example, a minority person may view affirmative action as equality but a white male might view it as loss of freedom, and a person with a low income may view progressive taxation as justice whereas a person with a high income sees it as loss of freedom and inequality.

The solution is to prioritize these ideals in order of importance. Certainly, justice and equality are important, but freedom is the highest ideal. Justice is important, but what use is it if one is not free to be just, and with equality, one may have the opportunity to be equal but not the freedom to be so. With freedom all the other ideals are attainable and without it they are meaningless, thus the other ideals presuppose freedom. For the purposes this book and the evaluation of socialism, it is not so critical how one ranks these ideals but rather that freedom is ranked first.

People do not appreciate the relative value of freedom until it is lost. Freedom is like health; it is taken for granted until gone, and then one can think of nothing else but getting it back.

The point is that socialism does not value freedom, it denies it. Socialism's ideology, which requires the state control of the means of production and distribution of wealth, takes freedom from the individual and gives it to the state. The socialist concept of "from each his ability" removes the freedom to keep the fruits of individual labor, and the requirement of "to each his need" imposes obligations on others. To succeed, socialism requires big government, high taxes and restrictions on individual freedom. The whole concept of socialism is based on collectivism, which is the antithesis of individual freedom; it means to give up freedom to the collective group. Freedom trumps socialism's equality and "social justice."

**Determinism vs. Free Will**

One way socialism takes freedom is by denying free will. Socialism dictates all humans are part of a collectivistic society, which brings inescapable and inexorable obligations and responsibilities. People are born into circumstances beyond their control. Individuals cannot choose their responsibilities; the responsibilities just exist—they existed before the individual arrived. Socialism maintains citizens are not individuals and do not have the right to use free will to decide whether to accept these obligations and duties. Citizens have no choice. Socialism is a deterministic philosophy that limits personal freedom.

Further, when socialism preaches "to each his need," it imparts a lethargizing force into society. In religious determinism people think to themselves "why try because the conclusion is determined. There is nothing I can do to change it." They resign themselves to fate, which attenuates their will to make things better. Similarly, in socialism, when the needy know their needs will be cared for, deterministically their will is enervated because it does not matter what they do.

Individuals have the right to freedom, the free exercise of their will and choice. They should have the freedom to choose their obligations and duties. They should have the right to choose whether to be part of the group or be independent. An individual has the right to be more than the group—to be different. One has, for example, the right to choose between socialism and free enterprise. One is more than others' definition of oneself; rather, each individual is a being who has the right to labor progressively for his or her own perfection unencumbered by a socialistic deterministic philosophy. A human has the right to make of oneself what one will. Deterministic socialism limits the individual's potential, defines that person and limits one's freedom.

## Freedom Defined

Socialists claim socialism brings freedom, but they confuse freedom with justice and security. Freedom does not necessarily bring justice, and justice does not necessarily come from freedom. True freedom has a downside. There must exist the possibility for negative consequences for actions to truly be free. The socialists want freedom to be all upside; they want it both ways. Socialist freedom thus becomes security because there is no downside. When they claim socialism brings freedom, they really mean it brings security.

Freedom does not come from the imposition of obligation on one to provide security for another. Socialism calls this security freedom but never mentions the imposition. To be freedom, it must be freedom for all. Socialism suffers an inherent contradiction in this respect because it purports to bring freedom only by oppressing some. It grants freedom by taking it away. One person's freedom becomes another's obligation under socialism. In the end, socialism is not about freedom, it about the restriction of freedom.

## Loss of Individuality

Closely associated with the loss of freedom is the loss of individuality under socialism. A person has the right to make choices, especially choices that may run counter to the will of the group. Under collectivism the individual will is subordinated to the will of the group and fate takes over. There exists a historic tension between individuals and the collective group over the ownership of people. Many institutions, such as religions and the state, endeavor to declare people subjects who are subordinate to the will of the institution. States, in particular, are prone to view citizens as a commodity, something to be owned, manipulated, directed, harnessed, used and taxed. States see individuals as a collective group whose primary purpose is to support the state. Socialist theory is especially inclined to this type of thinking.

Unequivocally, every person has the inalienable right to own oneself. Indeed, as in the case of individual freedom, it seems ridiculous to argue otherwise. Each person is one's own body, mind and soul. Each human thinks to oneself and directs oneself. Each is an individual with an independent will.

Socialism usurps the right of self-ownership. Socialism is collectivism, which sees citizens as a group, or aggregate, and not as individuals. Under socialism the state owns the means of production and distribution, not individuals. "From each his ability" means the individual must surrender the fruits of self-labor to the group. The individual cannot own property under extreme socialism; only the state has that right. The entire philosophy of socialism is imbued with obligations and responsibilities that necessarily take individual free will and freedom of choice. The ideology coercively limits and obligates the individual and attenuates individualism.

Under socialism, individualism must be diminished because when individuals are independent they are free to decide whether to join the group or not. They may decide, for example, not to give what they have earned to the needy, which would spell the end to socialism. Socialism must suppress individualism to function.

Socialist literature is replete with attacks on individualism. It refers to the *brutal reign of the individual, the ills of individualism and the worship of individualism as the desire to bring back white slavery.* Virtually all socialist countries suppress individualism.

People should have the right to decide for themselves whether to cooperate or compete. One has the right to be free, independent, self-reliant and an individual. Each person has the right to be free from the group, from group pressure and the requirements to conform in all things. Humans have the right to be themselves and not what a group wants them to be. Socialistic collectivism steals self-identity by defacing individuality. The socialist attack on individualism is an attack on the human spirit.

It is not hard to understand why socialistic societies based on collectivism ultimately fail. Individualistic societies are comprised of self-reliant, vigorous, enterprising, hard-working and entrepreneurial individuals. They are willful people who endeavor to gain control of themselves and their environment. They create wealth and do not rely on the government/group to support them. They are provident because they care for themselves.

A collectivistic society is different. It engenders reliant, dependent, attenuated and sometimes lazy people who expect the government/group to provide for their needs. These are pliant people who are controlled by their environment. They do not create wealth, and they rely on others to support them. They are often improvident because they are not responsible for their own care. Collectivism is a mentally and physically lethargizing force, and societies based on it are usually weak and lifeless. Such societies die a slow death under their own feebleness.

## Individuality vs. Collectivism

With the exception of some early associations we are born into such as family, people are individuals first. People are free individuals with the freedom to choose obligations and associations. This freedom of choice also includes the freedom to decide whether to be a socialist or not, a choice the socialists would rather none have. Socialism offers no exit option; it requires the individual to remain as a member.

There are two kinds of collectivism, one natural and the other artificial. Natural collectivism involves associations that come about naturally, like families or cooperative ventures (like hunting and farming) undertaken for survival. Gertrude Himmelfarb in her book *One Nation, Two Cultures* calls this group civil society. This is a natural community.

The other form of collective society is artificial. When socialism preaches "from each his ability, to each his need," the consequence is a forced and unnatural group. This formula forcibly makes one give to another. It is pressured cooperation because some individuals who may prefer not to join the association are forced to. This artificial collective imposes obligations and responsibilities. This type of socialistic cooperative association does not come from the inside; it is imposed from the outside—it is an enforced community.

The socialists use many different arguments to support this form of unnatural collectivism in order to support their ideology. One common claim is what an individual has today depends on someone before them who provided it who in turn received those benefits from the one before them and so on.

This argument is flawed for a number of reasons. First, it does not account for the many pejorative actions taken by one generation on another. Second, the web of benefits is not as strong as the socialists would like us to believe.

It is true that individuals do receive some benefits from previous generations and it is only right that these be repaid and that individuals should help support future generations. Paying for and providing for such things as education, roads, sewers, police and fire protection are legitimate. But this argument for socialism goes far beyond these basic services and requires each pay to provide for others based on need.

Socialistic totalitarianism, collectivism and coerciveness are undoing what our forefathers created. Indeed, socialism is subverting our forefather's intentions of limited government, low debt and low taxes. The socialists say on one hand that we all stand on the benefits conferred by previous generations, such as these from our forefathers, but then proceed to undo many of those conferred benefits.

Under this socialistic artificial form of community government must increase in size to provide according to people's needs. As it increases in size it takes increasingly more from some, which it gives to others. The government must force cooperation and compliance. It must necessarily become totalitarian, which only increases individual resistance. Government reacts by passing laws that attempt to legislate morality, and people resist these as well. As resistance builds, the government becomes even more coercive, threatening and menacing to achieve compliance. Gradually the cycle spirals out of control until a totalitarian socialistic government finds itself having to repress a sullen and non-cooperative citizenry simply to function. Tax evasion, black markets and crime are common in such societies. Himmelfarb made the point that this immorality inherent in the artificial group actually works to destroy the community. Ironically, artificial socialistic collectivism actually diminishes one's natural inclinations toward collective civility.

Perhaps the most important thing to remember about the value of individualism is that free and independent individuals are a society's best protection against a socialistic totalitarian state. In America, those who do not toe the Democratic, progressive and socialistic line are labeled politically incorrect, backward, arrogant and out of the mainstream. In extreme socialistic countries, like the former Soviet Union and Cuba, such people are simply jailed or shot. Individuality trumps collectivism for a number of reasons, but its ability to preserve freedom is the most important.

**Historically**

Human history is predominately a history of individuals being controlled by institutions, such as religion or the state. Many religious movements, such as the Reformation, and rebellions, such as the American Revolution, can be seen as people's efforts to throw off the chains of group dominance in an effort to be individuals. Socialism destroys humanity's progression to individualism and reverts one back to being a member of recidivist collective society. It is a regressive philosophy that nullifies any progress humans have made to free themselves from the oppressive nature of the collective group.

America represents humanity's furthest advance in the march to become individuals. This nation was founded on individual freedom, and its historic ethic is one of the rugged individual. This is the land of exuberant individualism, New England independence and the Wild West. Politically, one of the core ethics of the Jacksonian Era was individualism. Theodore Roosevelt was the epitome of the rugged individualist. Early America was the land of unlimited opportunities and possibilities for the individual. There is no question American roots are planted firmly in the ethic of individualism.

Ralph Waldo Emerson (1803-1882) was an original American intellectual who, perhaps more than any other historic figure, best expressed these sentiments about America's foundations. Emerson's philosophy was transcendentalism, which espoused freedom and autonomy. For Emerson the belief *begins with philosophic freedom and ends in democratic individualism.* In his essay *Self-Reliance* Emerson wrote about the *centuries which have conspired against the sanity and authority of the soul.* He rails against the coercive and collective group when he writes *you will always find those who think they know what is your duty better than you and do not tell me of my obligations to put all poor men in good situations.* He lashed out at collective society when he wrote *society draws out the sinew and heart of man and we become timorous, desponding whimperers afraid of fortune, afraid of death, and afraid of each other.*

Emerson admonished Americans to eschew the collective group and become individuals with the famous words *it is easy in the world to live after the world's opinion but the great man is he who in the midst of the crowd keeps with perfect sweetness the independence of solitude.* He progresses from independence to self-reliance with the words *it is only as a man puts off all foreign support, and stands alone, that I see him to be strong and to prevail.* He finishes with the personal declaration that *my life is for itself and not for a spectacle.* Emerson is describing the heart and soul of a strong, independent and self-reliant America.

Socialism militates against this independent individualist American tradition — socialism is not America's heritage.

## Philosophically

Emerson felt the highest virtue in any group must be conformity, which is a futureless situation for the individual. To enforce conformity, the group excludes and vilifies nonconforming individualists. The only way to survive and rise within the group, according to Emerson, is to conform. He wrote *society everywhere is in conspiracy against the manhood of every one of its members. The virtue in most request is conformity. Self-reliance is the aversion.*

Under socialism individuals have no value because they must conform. They are analogous to a cog in a huge socialistic grinding machine. The cog is entirely controlled by the machine — it has no ability to control itself. The very nature of the machine requires the cog to conform to its function and purpose. It is lost within the workings of a vast, inter-related and self-perpetuating organ that has little concern for its individual members. The cog must speed up when some-one hits the accelerator and slow down when another hits the break. It is entirely at the mercy of a large, amorphous and capricious system. It has no control over its fate and no free will. The cog's only value is to operate as a part of the machine — it has no value in and of itself.

For Emerson the machine is the sum of its individu-al cogs, and without them it is nothing. The group thrives by celebrating its individual members and allowing them the freedom to achieve their unique individual potentials. Emerson is a proponent for individuals owning themselves. This wonderful philosophy made America great and is the opposite of the socialistic collective imitative system.

This means socialism is at war with individuals' es-sential nature. Socialism does not fit the nature of humanity like capitalism and free enterprise. Capitalism harnesses hu-man's selfish inclinations, which is why it succeeds so well. Socialism must coercively repress essential natures, which is why it ultimately fails.

Socialism is an ideology without a soul, because souls are not collectivistic. Only people have souls — concepts do not. Socialism is a devil that steals the individual's soul and buries it in a massive, common and unmarked collective grave. Socialism's denial of these truths manifests in very odd ways that lead them to some very unrealistic beliefs, which will be discussed next.

# Unrealistic Ideology

Socialism is an unrealistic philosophy that does not accommodate human nature, which makes it an ideology incapable of succeeding on its own merits. Reality's round hole will not accept its ideological square pegs. Socialists are utopian thinkers forever imagining places everyone desires but that do not and cannot exist; places where there are no worries, plentiful food and shelter for all. They imagine a place of beauty and warmth where all pleasures are to be had and all desires are fulfilled. Who would not want such a place? The problem is no such place exists except in the fabulist socialist's imagination. The truth is people must deal with what they have here and now and make the most of it.

Socialists selectively filter information that describes how things are so the information conforms to how they want reality to be. For example, it is unrealistic to assume people will work to their ability when they have no incentive, and the integrity of any society can be maintained when people are taken care of "according to their need." Neither accounts for human indolence, ambition or the need for accountability in society. Many socialists like Marx conceive utopian ideals in a vacuum and then endeavor to implement them through social engineering. When their ideals do not survive in the light of reality, socialists embark on a tortured and sophistic program of mental gymnastics in an attempt to justify their unrealistic idealized beliefs. Charles Fourier, for example, thought he could motivate people to work if they could pursue their passions. The consequence was the failure of his communal phalansteries. The truth is socialism cannot motivate people to work, and it certainly cannot persuade people to do the dirty jobs like empty septic tanks.

The unrealistic nature of socialism manifests itself in many ways. Following are a few of those manifestations in action and belief. It is unrealistic to attack the most able and productive of any society. Socialists, and especially many contemporary Democrats, attack the wealthy. Many of these wealthy are the most productive citizens of this country. Many facilitate America's production and distribution efficiently.

Businesses and especially corporations are also often vilified under socialism. They provide Americans access to food, shelter and autos; they pay millions in taxes; employ people; pay wages and dividends; and give Americans one of the highest standards of living in the world, yet socialists attack them. Ironically, because many socialists have never managed a business, they do not understand what it takes to successfully run one. They do not understand the volatile components that make for successful and efficient production including capital, interest, wages, employees, materials, unions, taxes, markets, methods and management.

Socialists are also naive and unsophisticated because they cannot tolerate the unequal distribution of wealth. It has been said the sophistication of any society is its ability to tolerate this unequal distribution, a sentiment that tacitly acknowledges the natural unequal abilities and talents of people. Individuals are unequal and the willingness to acknowledge and harness ability is good judgment; denying it is unrealistic and counterproductive.

The socialist denial of a natural order compounds many problems faced by humankind. Reality is a messy thing. Nature offers many natural disasters that introduce scarcity including famines, floods and pestilence. Nature maintains a natural balance between population and production, which is thwarted by the socialist creed of "to each his need." Under socialism, attenuating the fittest and perpetuating the least fit reverses natural balance. The consequences are overpopulation by the average, increased dependence and a society less able to deal with nature's scarcity. Thomas Malthus was vilified by English society for proposing the simple idea that any society that increases its dependent class will outstrip its own resources. Socialism's inability to acknowledge this truism is like denying people must breathe. The philosophy takes humans out of nature, which for some sounds good until the consequences emerge.

Socialism is also unrealistic in assuming humanity's problems are primarily economic in nature. Most socialists, especially Marx, consider economics both the source and solution of societal ills. But one does not live by bread alone. There are many reasons for civilization's ills, some of which are sociological, psychological, moral or environmental in nature, to name a few. Many ills are merely the consequence of human nature. Providing according to need without condition diminishes any social norms that require effort to be rewarded or imprudent behavior to be punished. If a person does not work they do not eat, but under socialism they do. Socialism removes personal responsibility by projecting individual problems on exterior sources—it blames someone or something else. It engages in confusing causes and consequences by disguising the real causes it cannot solve and replacing them with causes socialism purports to correct. Poverty becomes oppression by the rich, teenage pregnancy becomes lack of sex education, juvenile delinquency becomes the parent's fault, and crime, divorce and illegitimacy become society's fault. It is always someone else's fault but never the individual's.

Because socialism cannot accept human nature it must emphasize methods that purport to alter that nature. Socialists like Owen say a person is a product of environment so the person's environment must be changed.

Certainly, we are partly a product of our environment, but limiting it to that cause alone is unrealistic. Environment is only part of the equation. Parenting, education, social norms and individuals will also have much to do with character. The Puritan ethic of hard work and the capitalistic ethic of reward for effort incite good character. Ask yourself, what is the good character found within socialistic societies where the environment is ostensibly better? Castro, Hitler (Nazism is in part National Socialism) and Stalin and the environments they created are all products of socialist ideology and circumstances.

Education is one area socialists particularly emphasize. They believe education can change one's essential nature thereby making a good socialist; they think a person can be "educated" out of their human nature. This is unrealistic thinking and propaganda. It may be true some individuals can overcome essential natures through education, however, problematically, some people are dense, some lazy and others unwilling. In other words, some cannot learn to overcome their natures, some are unwilling to put forth the effort and some just stubbornly do not want to. Further, there simply are not enough resources to educate every man, woman and child on this earth to the point where they can renounce their natures and embrace socialistic doctrine. It is unrealistic for socialists to think they can change anyone's nature in any permanent or timeless way to accommodate socialist beliefs.

The most significant aspect of the socialists' proclivity to unrealistic thinking must be their unwillingness to accept the fact that socialism is incapable of producing wealth. Socialism cannot produce wealth, it can only distribute it. It could not produce wealth in the former Soviet Union, and it does not produce wealth in Cuba or Argentina. It makes no difference how socialists alter the means, the end is always the same: less wealth.

Some contemporary quasi-socialist societies, particularly Sweden, Britain and France, endeavor to resolve this problem by splitting socialism. To varying extents these countries' governments tacitly acknowledge socialism cannot produce wealth so they allow free enterprise to produce wealth, which socialism will distribute; they split production and distribution. They split the two and allow capitalism to handle production and socialism the distribution. This is clearly the height of socialistic unrealistic thinking. These governments are saying to those who are able, "You make it and we will spend it, we cannot make it, but you can make it, so you are obligated to make it for us so we can spend it. You work hard and we will take the benefits." It is like a wastrel husband saying it is his job, and right, to spend his wife's income. Socialism is good at spending money, which is the easy thing to do, but it is incapable of making money, which is hard. It can only distribute, not produce.

## John Stuart Mill

This socialist idea to split production and distribution was derived from the famous economist Mill. He proposed that *what a person has produced by his individual toil, unaided by anyone, he cannot keep, unless by the permission of society… the distribution of wealth, therefore depends on the laws and customs of society.* Socialists love this idea. It opens the door for them to redistribute wealth as they see fit because, according to Mill, the production of wealth is not dependent on its distribution. This idea is the basis for the modern welfare capitalistic states from America's New Deal to the socialistic Scandinavian countries. These states allow free enterprise and private property to control the means of production but distribute the wealth according to socialistic philosophy.

Nevertheless, Mill was concerned that even though societies may distribute wealth arbitrarily, they would ignore incentive *at their own risk.* Further, Mill feared any society whose distribution depended entirely upon the whims of a majority would diminish the individuality of character, make public opinion a tyrannical yoke and cause absolute dependence.

Subsequent economists have discredited Mill's unrealistic attempt to separate production from distribution. They maintain when a society intervenes in the distribution process it cannot help but influence production. A 100 percent tax on profits, for example, would certainly have a *terrific impact on how much there was, as well as on who got it.* Production is primarily a product of effort and enterprise, which come about by incentive. When a socialist society destroys incentive, it attenuates production. A society may, as Mill proclaims, distribute any way it wants, but there is a price to pay: there will be less to distribute. When the state takes the fruits of people's labor and destroys their incentive, they no longer labor, which makes socialism an unrealistic economic philosophy.

One theme throughout this book asserts that socialism is a parasitic philosophy — it is incapable of independent function and must have a viable host to survive. This charge is conspicuously demonstrated by the socialist effort to split socialism. Such efforts implicitly acknowledge socialism cannot produce, like a parasite, it can only exist by living off a host. The only way socialism can obtain anything to distribute is by sucking the wealth from systems capable of producing it, such as capitalism. Admitting they must split production and distribution collaterally demonstrates socialists' tacit acknowledgement that they are parasites, even though they are unaware of it.

This revelation demonstrates many of the charges against socialism. First, it is not a genuine self-sustainable economic system but rather a sentiment. Second, as an independent system, because it cannot create wealth, it only increases poverty. Third, this poverty necessarily brings with it debt and inflation when a socialist government spends beyond its means. Fourth, capitalism, free enterprise and private property are superior systems for wealth creation, which improves the social weal far more than socialism. Fifth, socialists are thieves because they do not produce but can only take coercively and without compensation. Finally, sixth, socialism is an unrealistic philosophy that fails on its own. The philosophy exists only by sucking the blood from its host, like a parasite.

## Elimination of Consequences and Loss of Personal Responsibility

Virtue is a condition of both freedom and justice. Humans enjoy freedom and justice only to the extent they control themselves. Without virtue there can be no freedom or justice. Accountability and personal responsibility are components of virtue; it is not enough to merely believe in virtue, a person must also act virtuously. To be free from theft, for example, one must not only believe it is wrong to steal but also not steal. Accountability and personal responsibility, therefore, are not necessarily the price of freedom and justice but rather the reward. Socialist philosophy fosters irresponsibility, attenuates personal responsibility and diminishes virtue. It does this from both ends. On one hand it weakens the most able's willingness to be virtuous, and on the other it weakens the feeblest's need to be virtuous. Socialism punishes virtue and rewards vice.

When socialism mandates "from each his ability," it neutralizes consequences and erodes personal responsibility. If the able person in a socialistic society works hard, the rewards for doing so are removed through progressive taxation. The consequences of working hard are detached from the reward or wealth; being industrious is no longer a virtue. The able are punished for effort. If the hard-working citizens report income correctly and honestly to the government, that information is used to tax them progressively higher, and the virtue of honesty becomes a liability. Many such virtues, including personal responsibility, which are preconditions to a virtuous society, are turned around under socialism and used against the able individual; virtues become vices.

When socialism mandates "to each his need" one does not have to work. They are no longer responsible and no longer suffer the consequences for their actions and decisions; they get something for nothing. They receive all the benefits without the effort and without having to, for example, pay taxes.

To make matters worse, when the weak or needy receive benefits without effort they appreciate the benefits less and demand more services. They appreciate it less because they did not work for it and demand more because someone else pays. The desire for something as long as another pays is a natural human inclination that cannot be overemphasized. Socialism feeds this inclination and is, in turn, supported by it. When people must pay for their own support they are naturally more cautious and providential. They usually restrain their spending and are more vigilant and self-limiting. These are some of the consequences when people are not held accountable or personally responsible under socialism.

Good decisions require accountability of one's actions, the experience of the consequences of those actions and one taking responsibility for the actions. Good decisions and actions are far less likely without accountability. Introducing consequences has a profound effect on people's fortunes. Much of what humans do as individuals create the circumstances that either help or hinder them.

Consider hypothetical individuals A and B. B is lazy, unfocused, lacks virtue and is dying from self-inflicted alcohol abuse. It is no surprise the person got a poor job, had a low income and is divorced and ill. Individual A, on the other hand, worked hard, was focused, had virtue and lives a healthful lifestyle. This person was rewarded with a good job, a high income, a stable family, marriage and good health. These two individuals' consequences were a result of the choices they made. Bad choices usually bring bad consequences, and good choices often bring good ones. These choices are innumerable; they can involve finances, personal lives, attitudes, beliefs, actions and relationships to name a few. Socialism changes all of this.

When socialism preaches "from each his ability, to each his need," it detaches the individual from the consequences of their actions. Socialism penalizes individual A by taxing them progressively more than it taxes individual B. The end result is individual A, under socialism, is made to support individual B. By doing this socialism penalizes the very person who contributes the most to society and rewards the one who contributes the least. It makes individual A responsible for individual B's bad decisions. It rewards individuals B's bad choices and penalizes individual A's good ones. Under socialism, individual B is rewarded for bad decisions, suffers no consequences for his bad decisions and is supported by others. Socialism is indeed a very strange and backward ideology.

These socialistic symptoms are seen in all aspects of American society today. Criminals escape personal responsibility with the insanity plea, children are not responsible for their actions because they have attention deficit disorder and people cannot control their weight because of their genes. Nobody is responsible for anything. Further, the judicial concept of damage is detached from justice under socialism. Rather than hold guilty parties responsible for their actions, the American judicial system allows the innocent to be sued because they may have deep pockets and are therefore able to pay. It becomes the tobacco company's fault when somebody smokes, the state's fault when a drunk driver runs a poorly lighted stop sign and the taxpayers who pay when a public employee is sexually harassed. Justice becomes expediency under socialism.

With the lack of accountability, the loss of personal responsibility and the diminution of virtue, it is no wonder black markets thrive, people avoid their tax obligations and the worst individuals rise to the top in virtually every socialistic society. Socialistic societies are virtueless and immoral.

# The Creation of Dependence

But it gets worse. Of all the manifestations of socialism, the creation of dependence is one of the most insidious.
Socialism creates dependent, other-reliant individuals and a
vast oscitant society of flaneurs. Under socialism, everyone
eventually becomes dependent on the state because the state
assumes the role of provider. It usurps the means of production and distribution of wealth so individuals no longer think
in terms of providing for themselves; they expect the state to
do it. People no longer look to themselves for solutions but
rather look to the state for answers. America today, under the
influence of creeping socialism, is creating just such a vast,
other-reliant and dependent citizenry.

As socialism captures more people in its web of dependence more become dependent—dependence breeds
dependence. When effort is detached from survival, people become dependent for a number of reasons. First, they
lose the understanding of what it takes to survive. They do
not know how much effort must be exerted to exist. They
come to take existence for granted and see their existence as
something to which they are entitled. Second, people do not
expend as much energy when they know personal effort is
not required to survive. They know the socialist state will
care for their needs regardless of how hard they work, or
whether they work at all.

On the other end of society's spectrum, the most productive and able are also gradually made dependent under
socialism. Because of the high confiscatory progressive tax

rates needed to pay for the government's socialistic programs, the able and productive citizens cannot save. They are prevented from creating any wealth that could facilitate independence, so they must also become reliant on the government. In America, savings rates plummeted during the 1990s. Personal savings as a percentage of disposable income was 7 percent in 1959 and today it is almost zero. Savings in America is at the lowest rate in national history. Americans no longer feel the need to save because they think the government will take care of them.

Socialism engenders a mentality of entitlement. People come to believe they are entitled to certain things. They come to believe they should be guaranteed a certain level of security. They become accustomed to socialistic governmental benefits programs, and, rather than view these programs as a temporary form of help, citizens increasingly demand benefits as permanent entitlements. People come to think they are entitled to a certain and guaranteed standard of living. They come to believe these things are their natural rights. However, these are only rights to the extent other people provide them. They are entitlements only because someone else works to provide the entitlement.

Socialism attenuates the historic American "can do," "go get 'em" and optimistic "pull yourself up by your bootstraps" ethic. The typical American family of the early 1900s thought "we must work to get money to survive and thrive." Such an attitude promoted productive, creative and self-reliant hardworking families with incentive. This attitude made the family responsible for its own fate. This attitude made America great.

The teachings of capitalism and socialism are analogous to two sets of parents with different ideas on how children should be raised. The first raises their children to be independent and self-reliant adults, so the parents impart the ethics that create such adults. They reward their children only after effort, they require the young adults to pay for their own auto insurance and insist on good grades before agreeing to help their children with college costs. The second parent set raises their children to be dependent and other-reliant adults. They give reward without condition, they pay for their children's auto insurance and they impart the idea that college is a right and not a privilege that requires good grades. Clearly, the odds are the first family's children will grow up to be strong, willful self-starters, while the latter become weak, expectant and needy. As it is the parents' eternal duty to raise children capable of living successful, independent lives, it is the state's responsibility to do likewise. Socialism totally fails in this respect because with its mantra of "to each his need" it creates citizens who are weak, expectant and needy.

Historically, self-reliance has been the rule. The Bible's admonition that it is better to teach a man to fish than give him fish is one example. If one is taught to fish the person can become self-reliant; if one is given fish the person will become dependent. The old proverb "empty sacks will never stand upright" is another example. Extreme dependence makes survival impossible. If the symptoms of poverty alone are addressed, the reasons for it will remain. To solve poverty one must address the reasons for it such as the attitudes that cause it. The sack must be filled with the right attitudes, beliefs and ideas. This is not to say those with extreme and temporary need should not be helped but rather the form of help should be engineered to make the recipient eventually self-reliant. It should teach them to fish and fill up their sacks with the right philosophies. Socialism does not do this. When socialism says "to each his need," it is blind. It offers the help without addressing the causes of the problem thus only perpetuating more need and creating more dependence.

Socialism creates a vast, needy, feeble and weak citizenry. There are no guarantees, entitlements or socialistic states in nature. Nature is indifferent to the human condition. The consequence, as Thomas Robert Malthus predicted, is an increasingly dependent, artificially created class which will outstrip society's dwindling resources and wealth.

## The Destruction of Incentive

There is an old tale of a Russian farmer who through years of hard work had built a nice farm and a comfortable life for himself and his family. Each spring the farmer had assiduously planted a new crop, which he would carefully tend during the summer and harvest in the fall. Each winter when the snow would accumulate and the cold winds would blow, he and his family would live well because of this harvest. The farmer had two neighbors who were not as industrious. They preferred to enjoy the summer at leisure and spend their time at the local pub. One especially cold winter the indolent neighbors nearly starved because they had failed to provision themselves for the winter. The next summer the farmer again planted his crop and prepared for the coming winter, while the neighbors again opted for the pub over their fields.

Things began to change that fall as the neighbors became concerned about surviving another winter with little food. They saw the industrious farmer's abundance and asked him if he would share his crop, to which he said no—he needed his stored food for his family. The neighbors called the farmer greedy and declared it immoral to let anyone starve. To correct this newly declared injustice, the improvident neighbors decided to form a democracy whereby the majority would rule. This they did, and the very first measure was to mandate the distribution of all harvests. The farmer was outvoted two to one in favor of splitting his harvest three ways. The farmer naturally was incensed, but there was nothing he could do about it. They all barely survived that winter because everyone was depending on one harvest. When spring came, it was time for the farmer to plant his new crop, but he had changed. He asked himself "Why should I work so hard on this crop when others who do nothing take two-thirds of the yield? Why not just relax and spend time at the pub like them?" He had lost his incentive to work. That fall there was no harvest to distribute and they all died of starvation during the winter.

This little tale may sound simplistic but it illustrates what happens under socialism. When socialism takes the fruits of one's labors it hebetates personal incentive. When a person's incentive is ruined, that which sustains one goes away. Socialism requires that each be provided for according to need like the neighbors in the Russian story. To do so it mandates the redistribution of wealth or the diligent farmer's crop. It makes no difference to socialists that the farmer earned his harvest, for them it is just a commodity to be redistributed according to need. It also makes no difference to socialists that the neighbors did not work; they are only concerned the needy may starve. It is a socialist formula for the decay of a society that has happened elsewhere, and it is happening in America today.

Socialists confuse greed with incentive. Incentive can lead to greed but not necessarily so. The farmer is not greedy for wanting to keep his harvest. By labeling incentive as greed for ideological purposes, socialists create one of the core reasons for their system's failure—it destroys incentive. In this respect, socialism does more than just suppress incentive; it also takes people's will—it destroys the will to achieve, thrive and survive. An individual comes into this world with hope, ambition and potential, which is systematically squashed by the socialist state. Socialism vitiates the human spirit.

Socialist Charles Fourier tried to address the problem of incentive in his communal phalanstery with an intellectual sleight of hand. He proposed people would work when work is for their pleasure or from their passion. Unfortunately, many find little pleasure in work, many are lazy and nobody wants to clean the septic tanks. Fourier attempted to overcome this problem by making his communes co-proprietorships with profit sharing, but this is just capitalism. Other socialists have tried to overcome this problem by attacking from other angles. Saint-Simon tried to master the problem of incentive with social cohesion, Proudhon with equality and liberty and the Fabians with happiness. Ultimately, none succeeded because their solutions are unrealistic and don't work.

The fact that virtually every commune established on purely socialistic ideology has failed is perhaps the best censure of socialism and in particular its proclivity to destroy incentive. For example, Fourier's followers in France started several communes and all failed. Some thirty-four Fourier-type communes were founded in America, the most famous of which was Brook Farm in Massachusetts, and all of these failed as well. Socialist Robert Owen's 1824 commune of New Harmony in Indiana failed because it ran out of money — and of course it ran out of money — nobody worked. Socialist Étienne Cabet's Icarian communes in Texas and Nauvoo, Illinois also failed. Every time a socialist commune fails socialists blame dissention, money problems, leadership, capitalism and even yellow fever. They blame everything but the loss of incentive. The truth is socialism fails because it destroys the incentive to work. It is a system that can only exist like a parasite within another system like capitalism. It is incapable of existing on its own.

William F. Buckley wrote that *those whose activity brings on a substantial rise in employment and in productivity ought not to be thought of as public enemies*. It truly is a strange ethic that attacks incentive and penalizes merit and a curious twist of mind that projects guilt for not paying enough taxes or for making too much money. This corrupt form of society systematically castigates and villainizes its most able and strong citizens, the tax-paying working class, and succors the non-working and non-tax-paying class. It is a strange and ironic society that reverses nature by penalizing success. It is a formula for a stagnant society.

**The Stagnation of Society**

Socialism does the same to the group that it does to the individual. It fosters lethargy because it removes reward for effort, reduces personal responsibility, reduces the individual and takes freedom. It is a system analogous to making decisions by committee. With rule by committee, the entire process of governing is weighted down with competing interests, lack of direction, lack of leadership and rules so diffuse there is usually little action and much confusion. Socialism, like a committee, is a system in slow motion totally bogged down by its own ponderousness.

Socialism breeds societal lassitude through its institutions and laws; little can be done or accomplished without mountains of bureaucratic paperwork and approvals. Its laws, which treat people unequally for social engineering purposes, depress many segments of society. Its morality, which denies any spirit of fairness, leads to resignation and frustration.

In the *Communist Manifesto*, Marx and Engels accused capitalism of *converting the physician, the lawyer, the priest, the poet, the man of science, into paid laborers.* They accused capitalism of stripping such citizens of their honored occupations and exploiting and reducing their personal worth and value.

This is nonsense. Capitalism and free enterprise, which are highly energizing societal forces, have created the opportunity for people in these occupations to thrive. Physicians, lawyers, priests, poets and scientists flourish in capitalist America far more than in any socialistic country. They have more opportunity to enter their respective fields, more opportunity to succeed, more rewards for succeeding and more success. Capitalist America, for example, has advanced medicine as well as some of the best doctors. The American capitalist system has created wealth that supports artists who, in turn, have created an explosion of innovation and new advancements in the arts. America is also technically and scientifically advanced due, in part, to the innovations of its scientists. Just think of the incredible inventions conceived under the American system such as the automobile, airplane, telephone and radio just to name a few. The energizing American capitalistic system itself has created the dynamic environment that allows these segments of society to achieve such towering success—levels of success far beyond any socialistic system.

The greatest disparity between capitalism and socialism that conspicuously displays socialism's lethargic nature is in the creation of wealth. Capitalism creates wealth and socialism does not mainly because it fails at production. Production is inherently an energetic process. It requires enterprise, innovation, boldness and risk, all of which socialism discourages. All socialism can do is take from some and give to others, which is mostly a negative process. Socialism both diminishes incentive by appropriating wealth through coercion and engenders a vast, dependent and languid population. Indeed, one only need compare East Berlin with West Berlin, the former Soviet Union with America, China with Hong Kong, North Korea with South Korea or most any former East Bloc countries with their Western counterpart to demonstrate this point.

Socialist disparagement of competition is a significant reason for being a lethargizing force. Socialists discourage competition and champion cooperation. Socialist literature is full of attacks on the tyranny and anarchy of competition that *assures the happiness and comfort of a few at the expense and suffering of the many*. However, competition is one of the energizing forces that drives capitalism and make it so successful. When people compete they work harder, produce more and conceive of new and better ideas. Competition has been the engine behind many of America's great achievements and advances. Competition brings out the best in a person's abilities, which propels societies to new heights. This is to everyone's advantage and not just a few.

Socialism's disparagement of competition is analogous to discouraging baseball because it is competitive. The game should not be played because one team will lose or someone will have to sit on the bench and not be able to play. Such logic proposes baseball is a wrongful sport because it encourages the *happiness and comfort of a few [players] at the expense and suffering of the many [non-players]* and that baseball should be discouraged because some do not play as well as others. This is ridiculous. Baseball is a game of competition, and without competition it would not be a game but rather some meaningless activity. Further, much of the vigor in baseball comes from competition, without it the game becomes a largely passive activity of merely hitting balls, running bases and chasing flies. Sports would not be sports and a society will not be vigorous without competition.

Competition also entails freedom. It is both the freedom to compete and fail as well as the freedom to decide whether to compete or cooperate. Freedom has a downside, which is the potential for failure. If a person is free to compete, they are also free to fail. When an individual makes the decision to compete, they collaterally accept the potential for failure. Socialism does not accept the downside of freedom because socialists want to eliminate failure. Therefore, they limit freedom and in the process the individual's right to choose whether to compete or cooperate. Socialism endeavors to replace individual competition with cooperative collectivism; it wants to force humanity to cooperate.

Finally, socialism is a lethargizing force because it attenuates will and personal responsibility. Earlier it was stated that under socialism people take less responsibility for their actions. In America today under the influence of socialism it is common for people to blame their problems on their circumstances or environment. It is always someone or something else causing their problems. Their circumstances are always due to some uncontrollable factor and the solution is invariably to be provided by someone else, which is usually the government. This formula destroys optimism, effort and "can-do" "pull yourself up by your bootstraps" attitudes. These positive attitudes are succored by a culture that encourages people to use their will or the ability to motivate oneself to do something. Socialism discourages this attitude and thereby creates stagnant societies full of stagnant people.

## The Destruction of the Ethic 'Reward for Effort'

Successful enterprises reward effort. Schools, companies, sports teams and states succeed by encouraging and rewarding superior performance. They are imbued with the ethic that hard work will be rewarded. People respond to challenges that offer reward and perform to their best ability. People want to get ahead, be recognized and secure wealth and security, and they will endeavor to attain these things if given the opportunity. Capitalism is successful at wealth creation partly because it accommodates this desire of people. Capitalism harnesses a person's natural inclinations and helps the individual succeed. Socialism does the opposite.

Socialism destroys the ethic of reward for effort in a number of ways. First, when socialism destabilizes or eliminates private property it removes a significant reward. People cannot be motivated to do their best when they cannot enjoy the fruits of their labors.

A second way is by discouraging wealth. Socialists disparage those who have made money and criticize those who enjoy the money they have made. What good is it to earn a reward that cannot be used? The socialist plague discourages the concept of having earned something. Anything over and above one's need is often not considered personally earned but rather community property. Recall socialist John Stuart Mill's words that *the distribution of wealth depends on the laws and customs of society.* Much of socialist literature decries the disparity of wealth, which carries the implication that if an individual has more than anyone else that individual is wealthy and to be disparaged. Earned wealth is a manifestation of success and should be encouraged. People should be allowed the freedom to take pride in what they have accomplished. If someone has worked hard and acquired a nice house they should not be made to feel guilty living in it.

Thirdly, socialism actively penalizes effort. Socialistic policies of progressive taxation and redistribution of income punish effort. The harder one works the more the government takes. Think how strange and backward this ethic is: the harder one works, the more successful one is, the more one is penalized. The New York cabbie who works sixty hours per week pays proportionately more in taxes than the one who works only forty hours each week. The harder worker is penalized for working more hours.

Finally, socialism attenuates the connection between effort and satisfaction. Most people feel satisfied with a job well done. When one builds a house, writes a book or raises a crop, that person can take satisfaction in having created something worthy; something personally created and sometimes personally owned. Socialism discourages individual ownership and replaces it with communal ownership. The connection between effort and reward is severed, and the individual cannot take pride of accomplishment or ownership. This socialistic elimination of satisfaction also manifests itself in government make-work jobs to keep unemployment down so common in socialistic countries like Sweden. Socialist Charles Fourier referred to this as *cultivating roses and gathering cherries*, but workers under these circumstances know their efforts are not genuine and that the program's purpose is to make work and not fill demand. What the workers create may have little value, so they take little satisfaction in their work.

## Socialism and Poverty

Of all the motivations for socialism the desire to end poverty has been unquestionably the most powerful and consistent. Many of the early utopian socialists like Robert Owen and Louis Blanc as well as members of the Fabian Society were motivated by the desire to alleviate poverty. This is a laudable goal, but consider the reasons for poverty.

There are many causes of poverty, some due to the individual and some to circumstance. For example, a person may be poor because of laziness and a refusal to work. The individual by choice is the source of the poverty. Another individual may be poor because the family breadwinner was killed in an auto accident and the survivor must bear the burden of supporting a family alone. This person is poor because of circumstance. Many people have little sympathy for the former but would like to help the latter.

Most sources fall into a vast, in-between gray area. These could include choosing a low-paying job, a farmer experiencing repeated weather-related crop failures, a divorced mother whose husband left because of her adultery, high medical bills for a terminally-ill lung cancer patient who smoked, the inability to get a job due to mental or physical disability or medical bills for an individual who was driving recklessly.

A significant weakness of socialism is that it does not distinguish between these sources of poverty. All that is required is that a person is in need. Because of this socialistic society are havens or places of safety and refuge for those who do not want to work, which makes the socialist blanket desire to alleviate poverty blind.

## Socialism Brings Misery

Many utopian socialists believe the goal of socialism is to bring the greatest happiness to the greatest number of people, which is another of its weaknesses. This is Jeremy Bentham's utilitarian philosophy.

There are three serious problems with making happiness an end in itself. First, happiness means different things to different people. What brings happiness to one may bring unhappiness to another. One may consider living in a shack in the country splendid while another views it as poverty. Second, happiness is an elusive concept. Many people spend their lives looking for happiness but never find it. Happiness is a very personal state of mind; in the end the only one who can bring happiness to fruition is the individual. Third, is it really one person's responsibility to make another happy? It is a real stretch to obligate one person for another's happiness.

Bentham's theory on utilitarianism has its limitations, especially when applied to socialism.

Also, like poverty, socialism does not distinguish between the various sources of misery. When socialism says "to each his need," it means that the miserable lifelong alcoholic who cannot afford a liver transplant is worthy. Socialism would require the state to pay for this transplant because the patient needs it. In a society free from this socialistic admonition, individuals are free to choose, based on circumstances, who is worthy of help and who is not. Socialism takes that freedom of choice away.

## Socialism Fails to Distinguish Need and Types of Help

It should be pointed out that there are also different types of help for those in need. Some help is contingent, short term and less expensive. This form of help gets someone through a rough time. Other help is incidental, a one-time occurrence and more cost effective. This form of help often has the effect of alleviating an immediate need and getting someone back on their feet. The final is guaranteed help regardless of causes.

Again, the problem is socialism makes no distinctions between any of these. Socialism lumps them all together and makes no effort to allocate or prioritize society's limited resources.

Socialists are always quick to point out poverty and misery in capitalist societies. Marx is notorious for this. In *Capital*, he criticized the accumulation of wealth in capitalistic societies because it caused *misery, agony of toil, slavery, ignorance, brutality [and] mental degradation at the opposite pole.* Socialists never acknowledge the misery created by socialism itself, especially when socialism develops to its logical conclusion, communism. As it turns out, the biggest problem in communistic countries is poverty and misery. There is poverty in Russia, China and Cuba, where few people could be described as prosperous and free from misery. In communism, the utilitarian theory of happiness for the most is turned on its head and becomes misery for the most. Bentham's theory becomes, in essence, destroy the happiness of many for the general misery and poverty of all.

## Emotion, Reason and Compassion

We would not be human without emotions. Along with the drive for survival, emotions are some of our most basic instincts. Love, anger, envy, fear, avarice and lust are the stuff of humanity. Indeed, any human without emotions could only be described as a psychopath. Unfortunately, socialism is an ideology that stirs one to excessive emotion and passion.

The problem is that passion can lead to lynch mobs. One can easily imagine two members of a mob in high excitement exclaiming the awfulness of the accused crime and the need for revenge and driving each other to action. These are feelings run wild, emotions out of control and passion. It is mob rule, and innocent people have lost lives because of it.

Humans have another quality, which is the capacity to reason. People have an intelligence that allows them to syllogize, reflect, evaluate and analyze. Some call it common sense. Many of the ancient philosophers observed the consequences of unrestrained emotions and proposed reason as the antidote. Many consider this higher faculty an essential human distinction from the animals and what makes humans special and elevates them from their crude animalistic natures. It is reason and not passion that has led to advanced concepts held dear today such as justice, equality and freedom, and it is these concepts that restrain the mob. Out of the passionate cacophony of the mob arises one wise soul who suggests that, in the name of fairness, the accused should be considered innocent until proven guilty, that judgment be based on the evidence and that a trial by jury should be held. The mob is admonished to control their emotions and mitigate their passions. The speaker is the voice of reason.

Indeed, it may very well be that the ability to control human emotions is what allows for cities, states and civilizations. This same reason should restrain the socialist passions of sympathy, empathy and pity. It should restrain excessive compassion.

Socialism incites the emotion of compassion in particular and specifically the compassion to alleviate suffering and misery. It is the passionate feeling of empathy for those in need and the desire to do something about it. But, like the lynch mob, it is compassion out of control. It is unrestrained emotionalism to the point of being maudlin. It is passion unchecked by rationality.

Socialists do not restrain their passions with reason, rather their passion acts like a horse blinder. They are so passionately desirous for an end they deny the consequences of the means. They do not know when to draw the line. When they see need all they can think of is meeting it. The poor will always be a part of society, and their needs are bottomless. Once a society begins on that socialistic slippery slope there is no ending until the society has spent its wealth. Socialists have no ability to restrain spending, to budget or to prioritize assets due to their voracious and unquenchable appetite for wealth. Recall socialist welfarist Bernie Sanders who wants to take wealth from the rich and create a welfare state.

Socialists do not have a monopoly on compassion. The conservative may have compassion and give, but if they do not give enough they are called cheap, mean, selfish and parsimonious. It is easy to be compassionate and it is hard, like a father, to say no, and anyone who says no is immediately vilified by socialists. Under socialism prudence becomes greed, thrift becomes selfishness and saving becomes hoarding. Socialists can always demand more compassion, but they can never bring themselves to ask where it should stop. They are incapable of restraining their compassion and drawing a line. Like the father who budgets and draws limits, the conservative is always the one who gets the disapprobation and the socialist gets the credit. Socialists garner the approbation for being generous, for being compassionate and for caring for the needy. This is one reason many politicians and most of the media are Democrats—compassion makes them look good, so they get good ratings or more votes. Their compassion trumps their reason.

Dealing with socialists is like dealing with a mercurial, emotional and irresponsible spendthrift. They are so driven by emotion most will not listen to reason. They are people like Marx and Saint-Simon who are incapable of living within their means. They are usually incapable at handling money and assets. They think if "I have it, spend it" without regard to future consequences. They usually think only in terms of short-term gains not long-term losses. They seem incapable of controlling their emotions or controlling themselves.

Naturally it is often those with the least to give who are socialists. It is easy for them to be compassionate because they are not the ones giving. It is always the other guy who must pay. It is easy to be compassionate when giving away what someone else owns. It is harder to be compassionate when one shoulders the personal responsibility. This socialist hypocrisy is made conspicuous by the observation that compassionate persons are always free to give all they want, but many do not. Rather, they agitate and vote for laws such as progressive taxation so the burden spreads to other people and not themselves. Similar to this group are the many rich socialists who can afford to be compassionate. They are wealthy, so giving is less of a burden while garnering the credit with little cost while others pay. Compassion also comes easily to those who have made it financially through pensions, Social Security or inheritance. They are secure financially, so there is little risk for being compassionate because they have theirs.

All these socialist groups miss the reality of many middle class individuals and families who are neither rich nor poor. These are the people working at jobs, struggling to make ends meet, budgeting, raising and paying for children, paying a mortgage and saving for college and retirement. These people do not have a safety net or guaranteed sources of income. These are the people who have to be prudential with their money and are paying the high taxes for the socialistic programs. These are the working people who socialism purports to represent. They are the kulaks of America, the working people, and usually the bulwark against the plague.

## Reason vs. Intuition

In a similar way, socialism emphasizes intuition over reason. Ralph Waldo Emerson once wrote *thinking is the hardest thing to do, that is why so few do it.* Socialists usually think with their intuition and not their reason. They make decisions based on how they feel or what their gut tells them. They are typically emotionally driven people who lead emotionally driven lives. Decision making by intuition and not reason leads to many pejorative consequences. For one, intuition may lead to good decisions for the individual socialist but not necessarily for everyone else — what is good intuitively for one person may not be good for another. When socialists endeavor to impose their intuitively better decisions on others, the consequences are necessarily coercion, intolerance and totalitarianism.

Intuitive decisions are also often the furthest from reality. Individuals interpret reality differently and therefore may have different intuitive feelings about things. Who is to say which intuitive feeling is better? This leads to another problem with intuition, which is that it is almost entirely subjective. The premises for the decision are rarely known objectively, so the conclusions are often capricious. How does one debate with a subjective and capricious intuitively derived opinion?

Because of these problems, reason rarely persuades socialists. They just know what is right. They just know down deep that non-socialists are wrong. This is why socialists are so intolerant and explains why many artists are socialists. Actors mine their emotions and use their intuition for dramatic effect, painters dig deep down to express themselves on canvas, and poets use their intuition to express feelings in verse that are inexpressible in prose. They are all communicating in the language of feeling that is fine in art but scary in politics and government. Building a political system on intuition is like building a house of straw — it will not withstand the winds of reality.

Intuitively and emotionally driven people are some of the worst kinds of people to run a state. They are often fey, undependable, fickle and unsteady. They seem to thrive on emotion, are easily swayed by fashion and are often self-indulgent. Too often they are some of the most immoral people without scruples or probity. They sometimes self-righteously believe themselves to be above morality as if it is a concept only for other people. Some complain of middle class morality that they consider below them. They are the idealists and the dreamers. They are often the furthest from reality, and it seems the further they get the more liberal and socialist they become. They are people who think with their hearts, emotions and passions and not with their minds. They are the ones who were idealists in college with a heart and never changed. They are the ones who, when they graduated from college and got a job, never became conservative because they did not have a brain. They are the susceptible emotionally driven members of a lynch mob.

Socialists' intuitive decisions are too often inconsistent, which leads them to some very odd and strange contradictions. Their reasoned brain is at war with their impassioned heart. The predictable result is that socialists' mouths have two masters and can only speak in confusing and contradictory ways. They begin to expound oxymora like managed competition, individualistic collectivism, free planned societies and democratic socialism. Recall Bernie Sanders preferred to be called a welfarist rather than a socialist hoping voters will discern a difference. Their words become progressively confused and their thinking increasingly tortured. Their muddled thinking crowds out any hope for clear-headedness. In the end contradictions abound and reason, along with their brains, takes flight.

## The Diminution of Ambition

Similar to incentive discussed earlier, ambition is good, but socialists call those with it greedy. The charge usually breaks down into two accusations, one specific and the other general. The specific objection is that greed is itself a pejorative human desire. Greed is selfishness incarnate, and when people acquire and horde beyond their immediate needs, others are left in want.

The second objection is general in nature. To socialists, greed as a motivator is itself wrong. The health of a society should not be based on selfish motives. Adam Smith's invisible hand, which describes free markets as individuals, each pursuing personal selfish interests is the wrong foundation for any society. They believe society should be focused on cooperation and sharing and not competition and accumulation. Socialists see one conspicuous manifestation of this type of greed in the profit motive. Corporations in capitalistic societies survive by making a profit. Socialists believe profit devalues other considerations such as sharing and cooperation. They think when greed and money prevail, human values go out the window and the pursuit of money replaces human values. Philosophically, society should not be built on self-interest and greed but rather sharing, collectivism, cooperation and community for the alleviation of human suffering.

The motivations for and answers to these socialistic concerns are complex. However, if the artificial socialistic filter to reality is removed, a more realistic perspective emerges. As it turns out, the socialist's use of the term greed is narrow and extreme, capitalists are generous and socialists are the greediest people of all.

First, the socialist use of the term greed is an exaggeration. Sharing is a continuum from most to least beginning with altruistic and then munificent, generous, sharing, provident, selfish and greedy. Socialists ignore these levels of sharing. Someone may, for example, not share much because they are provident. They want their taxes low because they want to save for the future or they desire financial securi-ty. They are just careful. Understandably but ironically, the generous poor person will most likely give less than the rich selfish one. Socialists lump everyone together and call them greedy. They make no distinctions nor do they account for the magnitude of benefits from the "selfish" rich. Provident people who want to keep their money or rich people who give little are all called greedy. Socialists are extremists in their use of the word greed.

Second, socialists confuse greed with incentive. The world is competitive and, unless one is a socialist, one does not get something for nothing. Nature demands that people work to survive. Most people naturally have the incentive or ambition to survive. These motivations are honorable and not greedy. Individuals may want financial security, to save for college or retirement or just to buy a nice house or car. Many desire to go beyond simple survival and enjoy some of the better things in life. They may prefer steak to hamburger or a fine wine rather than beer. These are not bad things but rather people endeavoring to fulfill their desires, support their families, attend to their security or just enjoy life, tasks the socialists make more difficult. Because these people want these things for themselves, socialists call them greedy. In one stroke the socialist brush wrongly paints ambition and incentive the same ugly greedy color.

The American dream is one of getting ahead. This nation is the land of opportunity where people can succeed through hard work. The American tradition is one of rags-to-riches success based on effort. Neither the older aristocratic nor socialistic societies offer such an opportunity. In aristocracies a few are born with privilege, and in socialistic societies ambition is discouraged and there are few materialistic privileges to be had. America has evolved beyond both of these alternatives and rewards ambition and uniquely offers the opportunity to succeed. The socialists label this ethic as greed and vilify those who dream the American dream.

Consider the Erewhonian logic of the socialist's position. An ambitious person works hard and makes a high income, which is progressively taxed at 40 to 50 percent, which in turn pays for most government programs and benefits for the non-taxpaying poor, and then the ambitious person is called greedy by the socialists. Moreover, when the high tax bracket individual gets more money back in tax breaks or credits because more was paid in, socialists label it handouts to the greedy rich or welfare in the case of corporations. Realistically, these ambitious people are the most generous because they are the ones paying for most of the socialistic governmental welfare programs. These are also the people who are the most self-reliant and least likely to require any governmental assistance. It is all a one-way street in which they pay the government and get little in return. It is also these self-reliant people who, when they have a surfeit of wealth, often give much of it away. The working families, corporations and the very wealthy contribute more in time and money for social programs and philanthropic endeavors than most other segments of society. The socialists vilify the very people who pay and support their cherished social programs. They call them greedy.

In order to counter the socialistic accusation that the wealthy are greedy, a national tax grading system could be instituted. Such a system could grade citizens on the amount of taxes they pay. The more the taxes the higher the grade and the greater the societal approbation; conversely, the lower the taxes the lower the grade and the greater the disapprobation for not contributing enough to society.

There are a few interesting observations this system would make conspicuous. First, the socialists, and in particular the Democrats, would never agree to such a system because it would demonstrate their hypocrisy. Their claim that the rich don't pay and that they are greedy would be shown to be false. Second, even if the system were voluntary, they would object because those that refused to participate would be tainted. It would be a tainting similar to those that plead the Fifth, thereby refusing to cooperate with any legal questioning. Third, it would put the spotlight on those who pay little or no taxes and contribute the least to society. Specifically, those socialists with low grades that demand more governmental benefits and services would be exposed. And finally, such a system would give credit to those that pay the most.

A much stronger case can be made that socialists are greedy. Socialists advocate federal programs that greedily take individuals' money and increasingly consume the wealth of the nation. Since 1993, federal tax receipts in America have grown 52 percent faster than personal incomes, and since 1998 80 percent faster. The poor increasingly and greedily vote for socialistic wealth redistribution programs for their own benefit. They take money others earned. Unions greedily lobby and strike for higher wages and benefits. Democrats greedily clamor for higher progressive taxation. Socialists greedily demand that wealth be redistributed and industries nationalized. Captured socialists greedily vote to insure that their entitlement programs are maintained. These socialists are not only greedily grasping for wealth but also depriving others of the fruits of their own labors. It turns out that the socialists are the greediest of all.

To make matters worse, socialism has no self-correcting mechanism for its own greed. Competition in capitalism automatically corrects greed. If a company charges too much for its product or service someone else will offer it for less. Competition prevents gouging, overcharging and greed. The capitalistic corporate profit motive is a gauge of a corporation's success. Gouging may bring short-term benefits but in the end competition will reduce profits and put corporations out of business. When describing the philosophy of Adam Smith in his book *The Worldly Philosophers*, Robert L. Heilbroner put it this way:

> A man who permits his self interest to run
> away with him [in a free market system]
> will find that competitors have slipped in to
> take his trade away; if he charges too much
> for his wares or if he refuses to pay as much
> as everybody else for his workers, he will
> find himself without buyers in the one case
> and without employees in the other.

Socialistic governments have no such check because they have no competition. They operate outside of market forces like a monopoly and greedily raise taxes, consume wealth and spend indiscriminately. The socialists focus on government precisely because it is the only vehicle capable of satiating their greed.

By labeling ambition as greed and a commodity that needs to be contained, socialists slit their own throats. What they are really doing is collaterally containing ambition. This makes their ideology unrealistic, backward and ineffective. The truth is people are motivated by self-interest. People want to succeed and acquire property. When the ambition for success is labeled as greed then the rewards for effort are attenuated. People naturally will be less inclined to work, produce and become self-reliant—they become less ambitious. Unlike capitalism, the socialistic economic philosophy does not harness the natural inclinations of people. Under socialism the economic system is constantly at odds with the producers' wishes and desires. The socialistic desire to contain ambition is just unrealistic.

Socialists see society as a web of interconnected responsibilities and "gives and takes." If one has a surfeit of wealth and another is in need, socialists think the capitalist dam should be opened so the river of wealth may flow to the needy. The dam is greed and the flow is generosity. Socialists think it is fluid, but the flow always goes one way, with the ambitious supporting the needy. It is never reciprocal; the water never flows uphill to the reservoir. Socialists only see the world as the river flowing one way and ignore the benefits of the industry that created the dam. *Just breach it* is their ignorant cry. Once breached, the water storage and electrical benefits of the dam are lost until capitalist industry replaces them once again.

Many see themselves alone in this world and not dependent on anyone else. If they work and enjoy a surfeit they appreciate their good luck. If they fail they expect to suffer. They do not expect society to be obligated to them. This is not greed, it is self-reliance. Socialist greed reverses this philosophy and rewards indolence with "to each his need" and punishes effort with "from each his ability." The socialist forces the individual into their giving web or web of greed. Socialist ideology is backward because it calls the self-reliant and most productive greedy when in reality it is the reliant and least productive who are greedy.

Socialism is ineffective because it destroys incentive and ambition, relegates work to toil and removes any hope of advancement. Unlike capitalism, the plague offers no rewards for effort, denigrates the signs of success and labels ambition as greed. Where capitalism offers opportunity and hope, the plague only offers servitude and toil. Capitalism effectively harnesses human nature with free markets and competition and the consequence is a cornucopia of wealth. Robert Heilbroner captured this idea when he wrote:

> [T]he drive of individual self-interest in an environment of similarly motivated individuals will result in competition...

competition will result in the provision of those goods that society wants, in the quantity that society desires, and at the prices society is prepared to pay.

Socialism destroys all of this with its effort to contain greed, and its economic philosophy is stunningly and egregiously backward, unproductive and ineffective.

## Empty Security

It is natural for humans to want to be secure. People desire security in their personal lives, emotional lives and economic lives. Most want stable and secure personal lives, to avoid the sources of emotional angst and to be secure financially. These are only natural desires. Socialism exploits these natural human desires for security. When socialism offers that each shall be provided "according to their need" it purports to offer comprehensive economic security. It offers security in benefits such as Social Security, welfare, food stamps and rent subsidies. It also enshrines economic security in the law with such things as right-to-work laws, minimum wages and government make-work jobs. Contemporary catchphrases such as 'no child left behind" and "safety net" are manifestations of this socialistic promise of economic security. Socialism is about guaranteeing economic security, a guarantee many find irresistible.

This is a false and temporary kind of security. Socialist security is a security derived from the idea that "I am secure as long as you work," a security that depends on others' efforts. It is a tenuous security that is guaranteed at others' expense and a security that only lasts as long as the one who provides it continues to expend the effort to provide it. When those providing the security stop working, there is no more security. Under socialism it is the most able and productive citizens that provide the wealth that enables the socialistic government to offer security.

As will be seen, less is produced as the dwindling numbers of able and productive are increasingly harnessed under socialism. When less is produced, the socialistic society and the guarantees of security it offers become increasingly tenuous. As proof consider the securities offered in most socialistic countries. There was little security in the former Soviet Union when the food shelves were bare. There is little medical security in Cuba because although it offers free health care it is not as good as advanced countries' such as America. Under socialism there was no security in Argentina because their currency was worthless. Finally, the securities offered in Sweden are being threatened because the country's economy is precarious. These socialist offerings of security are short-term and empty promises.

Unlike socialism, the best security is the security one creates for oneself because the security provided by others could dissipate. Rather than relying on another's tenuous efforts to provide security, it is better to rely on one's own certain efforts because then there is control of effort. Individuals can determine how hard they want to work or how proficient they wish to become and consequentially how profitable they are at their livelihood. True security comes from the individual's efforts as well as saving, being providential, investing wisely (both doing and learning how to) and starting a business or learning a trade. Ultimately, one's security depends on oneself, not someone else. A self-reliant person is the most secure of all.

There are other reasons why socialism offers little security. First, under socialism it is the central planners who decide who gets what according to "to each his need," and not the marketplace. The planners' decisions balance different groups' conflicting claims for security. They must decide who is to be paid what, how much, whether you can get an apartment and who is to be allowed to enter certain jobs or trades. The consequence is security becomes politicized and the society's highest priority as the different groups jockey for more security. Nobody wants to be left out in the cold, so security becomes a commodity for which people must compete (ironically like capitalism but with fewer rewards). However, there is a difference. In capitalism to achieve security, one's success depends on oneself — in a socialistic society, one's ability to achieve security depends on someone else. Under socialism people have relinquished the freedom to succeed on their own merits. They have made a Faustian bargain; they gave up their freedom for a security that does not exist.

Second, socialism is incapable of production, which means that there will be dwindling wealth and consequently less security the state can offer. It is obvious that any system that offers security it cannot deliver is making an empty promise. Socialist states are like empty warehouses and efficient delivery systems that have nothing to deliver. This decline in wealth only exacerbates the desire for security as the competing groups find themselves disparately fighting over a decreasing supply. Ultimately, there is less security under socialism for everyone except perhaps the socialist leaders like millionaire socialist Bernie Sanders.

Third, socialism makes many less secure with higher taxes. When a government takes 30 to 50 percent of a citizen's income, it makes that individual less secure. That individual has less money to buy food, clothing, housing and less money to save for retirement. It makes it harder for the citizen to make ends meet. Rather than advocate an increase of an individual's security by lowering taxes, socialist Democrats do the opposite. They advocate higher taxes for more benefits, which only makes many taxpayers less secure. The socialist concept of security through taxation is indeed a strange one.

Socialism is a philosophy that denies the individual the opportunity to create for themselves the ultimate form of security because it prohibits or discourages the individual from creating personal wealth. People cannot legally create their own personal security under socialism. It transforms the individual's ability to become self-reliant into other-reliant; it makes individuals reliant on the state. Consequently the issue of socialism is very much an issue of freedom versus security. The question becomes deciding what is more important, freedom or security? This is a question that cannot be emphasized enough. Freedom and security are tradeoffs because giving more of one takes from the other and vice versa. For example, abolishing the automobile could prevent all deaths due to automobile accidents. If driving was outlawed the freedom to drive would be lost, but all would be perfectly safe from being injured in an auto accident. But people would lose the freedom to drive. In reality people prefer to risk security in exchange for the freedom to drive. Under socialism, like the freedom to drive, freedom loses to security.

Sadly, as a society such as America's comes to take its freedoms for granted, the people become increasingly willing to exchange freedom for security. They do this for a number of reasons. First, most forget what it is like without freedom. Second, as one group gains more security under socialism other groups become less secure, which drives their demand for security. Third, many falsely believe they can have both. They delude themselves into thinking that other people will willingly sacrifice and work for their security. The consequence is that for most citizens under socialism freedom is sacrificed at the altar of security. Freedom comes to mean little and security becomes their freedom. Benjamin Franklin described these people well when he wrote that *those who would give up essential liberty to purchase a little temporary safety deserve neither liberty nor safety.*

Finally, it is important to understand that security leads to dependence. When the individual's security is met by the socialistic state, that individual becomes dependent. As more citizens become dependent there are fewer producers, fewer goods and services and less security.

# *Chapter Four*

## Arguments That Relate To Society

The second set of arguments against socialism relate to society. Each of these arguments is summarized as follows.

### Injustice and the Rule of Law

It is important to understand the relationships between injustice, law and socialism. *Black's Law Dictionary* defines the rule of law as *the supremacy of regular as opposed to arbitrary power.* Other sources describe it as authority from the law and not governmental officials. For most of history there was no rule of law. Laws came from sovereigns as commands and were intended to further their interests. This form of law was often capricious, arbitrary, coercive and unjust. They were commands that ruled by brute force. To remedy this, humanity evolved the rule of law, which replaced sovereign commands with objective written standards, or laws that even the sovereign had to obey. Although there have been many interpretations of the evolution of law, it must be inferred the underlying motivation for the evolution to the rule of law was precisely the wish to make it less capricious, arbitrary and unjust. It was an effort to make law predictable, universal and fair. Socialists have abandoned this standard. They have come to view the law as a tool for social engineering necessary to create a socialistic state. Indeed, socialism views democracy and the laws it promulgates as its vehicle to success. The consequences are not only historically regressive but have created a body of capricious, arbitrary and unjust laws in America. An unjust, arbitrary and capricious socialist-inclined majority is legally tyrannizing many Americans, as Tocqueville predicted in *Democracy in America*.

Law must be based on some form of morality and in particular justice. First, it is simply the right thing to do. If people are to be compelled, that compelling force should be just. People have the right to be treated fairly and equitably by their government. Indeed, the Fourteenth Amendment to the Constitution requires the government to provide each of its citizens equal protection under the law. Many in Nazi Germany no doubt believed that anti-Jewish laws were satisfying and beneficial but they were bad laws because they were unjust. Second, laws must be just to gain people's voluntary compliance. If laws are unjust, law becomes arbitrary and coercive and people will endeavor to subvert it. Without morality law defeats its own purpose, which is to gain compliance. Laws that make most citizens lawbreakers are merely bad laws. Again, many of the citizens of Nazi Germany may have obeyed the law, but they did so out of fear.

Legal positivism is the view that the law is just a social fact unconnected to morality. This contemporary positivistic perspective of the law was precisely what Professor Hayek was referring to when describing the situation in Germany during the 1920s and '30s. It is this concept of legal positivism that detached the law from natural law in Germany then and is in the process of doing so in America today. In both cases the law becomes merely what authority says should be legal, reasoning that allowed the rise of Nazism in German. With legal positivism there are no limits to the power of the legislator or the government, and all traditions of limited government and citizens' fundamental liberties are lost. Socialism embraces legal positivism because it must pass unjust laws to bring socialism about.

Socialists have also reinterpreted the concept of justice with "social justice." With such an alteration they abandon the requirement that for something to be just it must be just for all. They desire to make justice selective, which is a hallmark of legal positivism. They claim that circumstances can require a remedy that does not treat everyone justly. This is simply not the case. True justice can never be achieved by committing an injustice. It may be true that justice is more than uniformity, but it is certain that it is no less than it. Justice, to be justice, must be timeless and universal and apply to all equally otherwise it is expediency. The socialist would deny this assertion.

In the case of socialistic progressive taxation, the one taxed at a greater rate committed no offense yet they are being treated differently, unjustly so. For any government to be called just it must treat all citizens uniformly, justly and equal under the rule of law.

The idea that laws must be based on justice is also closely associated with the Hobbesian concept of social contracts. Thomas Hobbes was also a proponent of natural law or law based on morality. Hobbes explained that individuals make contracts within a society; citizens voluntarily agree to limit their actions in exchange for others' similar commitments. For example, one agrees not to kill someone else in exchange for that person's commitment not to kill them. Contracts are like a fair bargain in which each voluntarily gives up something to get what they want. In the example above, the bargain is peace. Consequently, for these contracts to be valid, they must be based on some form of fairness, otherwise individuals would never voluntarily make or keep contracts. They are a form of negotiated justice and a prerequisite for any civilized society. Any civil society must base its legal system on this form of justice. It must endeavor to treat all citizens fairly and equitably. Socialism does not do this. Socialistic laws are utilitarian, unjust and break Hobbesian contracts. These utilitarian laws return citizens to the days when law was capricious and arbitrary.

Socialism directly violates the social contract. The socialists have bastardized this Hobbesian contract and now call it "the sacred social pact," a pact they endeavor to sanctify. But their pact is not a Hobbesian one because it is involuntary; many citizens, if given the choice, would not participate in it. Many, for example, would choose to invest their money into an IRA rather than Social Security. They know that their investment in the IRA compounded over many years far exceeds what they would receive in Social Security benefits. The socialists' "contract" is not a pact but rather the redistribution of wealth, and the "sacred social compact" is nothing more than a one-sided obligation from those who are able to provide for their retirement to those that cannot, do not or will not. It is a pact driven by the socialist ideology of "from each his ability, to each his need." It is an imposed obligation that limits individual freedom, commits injustice and violates the Hobbesian contract.

Socialism breaks this agreement in civility. It says "what is yours is mine." It is a concept not based on justice but rather on might makes right. The consequence is gradual societal disintegration because the contract is broken and the trust needed to support the contract is vitiated. Societal laws are no longer mutually beneficial but rather one-sided, coercive and unjust. Life under such legal circumstances necessarily becomes a power struggle, and the consequence is societal breakdown.

Because humans have unequal abilities, a socialistic state's laws endeavor to take from the endowed and deliver to the unendowed. It unjustly takes the property many have earned or accumulated, deprives the able of the fruits of personal labors and robs Peter to pay Paul. Socialism must therefore bring into question the ownership of any property a person may have. It must destabilize private property or ban it outright. Consequently, people are necessarily and unjustly deprived of their inherent right to own property. The concept of "mine" is not evil, it is natural and right. An individual has an inalienable right to keep what they have made or created, but socialism cannot allow citizens to own property because the state must own it to control production and distribute wealth. A state cannot distribute wealth it does not own, so it must usurp the right, thereby unjustly depriving some of their rights. The consequences are utilitarian laws based on social engineering and not justice. In layman's terms, it is legalized theft.

Under the plague's laws, there are many collateral unjust consequences in addition to the loss of ownership. Its laws discriminate, impose unfair obligations and deprive citizens of freedom and equal protection under the law. To illustrate these points, consider the following analogy. Under socialist dogma, a very strong man would be required to do the hardest physical jobs because he has the ability. His highest ability is strength; hence, he gets the hard jobs nobody else wants. However, what if the man prefers to be a lawyer? This choice is denied under socialism because the practice of law is not his highest ability. The socialistic philosophy that forces some to pay more because of an ability to pay is the same philosophy that forces an individual to a certain job merely because the person has a strong ability to do that job well. These souls have been unfairly obligated, their freedom has been curtailed, they have been discriminated against and they are not treated equally under utilitarian socialistic laws.

Such is the relationship between justice, law and socialism. Socialists use the law to bring about socialism, and the consequences are coercive and unjust laws. The worst of these socialistic unjust laws, progressive taxation, will be investigated next. First, however, to appreciate the enormity of progressive taxation and the damage it does to society, let us examine how Americans were taxed in the past and why socialistic ideology leads to progressive taxation.

## Non-Proportionality in Taxation

Two ways to apportion taxes are on the ability to pay or based on the benefits received. The former is based on the idea that the cost of government should be measured in accordance with an individual's wealth and income without consideration of the services or benefits one receives from the government. A progressive tax based on income would be one example of this method, and socialist ideology requires it. The second way asserts that each person's contribution to the government should be in proportion to the benefits one derives from the government. A road tax based on the amount of gasoline each driver purchases would be an example of this type of apportionment. In an ideal world, the obligation to pay in proportion to one's benefit is the fairest method.

America was founded on the basis that taxes should be proportional. Section 8 of the Constitution provided that all *Duties, Imports and Excises shall be uniform throughout the United States.* This meant all national taxes in the form of charges, including occupations, must be the same in all parts of the country. America's Founding Fathers were wary of big government and its potential for excessive and unfair taxation. The progressive socialist movement during the early 1900s did away with this quaint notion. Beginning in about 1900, pressure from the socialists, progressives and Democrats began to mount for a change in this fundamental American tenet. Agitation culminated in the passage of the Sixteenth Amendment to the Constitution in 1913 or the Socialist amendment, which changed the Constitution and gave the federal government the *power to lay and collect taxes on incomes…without apportionment among the several States, and without regard to any census or enumeration.* It opened the door for the federal government to tax people's incomes without apportionment among the states or division according to population. Without the Sixteenth Amendment, the income tax would have been levied such that the amount collected from each state would be in proportion to that state's population. The amendment opened the door to progressive taxation and the socialistic goal of the redistribution of wealth.

President Andrew Jackson once said *just laws make no distinction between rich and poor.* The socialistic amendment thwarted the Founding Fathers' intentions and allowed just such a distinction. It is only fair that one should pay for what they use, but it is unjust and coercive to make people pay for what they do not use. Non-proportionate taxation opens the door to socialistic social engineering and allows the socialists to become the arbiters of the society's wealth. They determine how much each citizen can earn, how much each can keep and where one's money will be spent.

The Sixteenth Amendment opened Pandora's Box and let socialism out. Federal income taxes immediately began to rise progressively after the passage of the amendment and the federal government grew exponentially. The socialists had secured the tool for social engineering. This social engineering peaked with the Revenue Act of 1954, which sharply increased the rate schedule but instituted deductions and exemptions. It further politicized the tax structure of America, further distanced taxation from the principles of proportionality and benefits received and laid the groundwork for massive injustice in the tax system. Predictably, today the socialists and Democrats endeavor to maintain the high progressive tax rates and eliminate any deductions or credits to corporations or the rich. America's tax system has become the captive of politics and in particular socialistic ideology.

Socialists often claim the wealthy are not paying their fair share of taxes. They make this claim when, in reality, it is the middle class, which includes some of the rich, who are paying the most for government and getting the least in return. It is curious the socialists never complain about the poor not paying their fair share. The poor pay little or nothing in taxes and get many benefits without cost. There exists no proportionality in taxation with regard to the poor, a fact socialists ignore. Why not let people individually choose which government services they want and then charge only for those services chosen? Such a system would be highly democratic, fair and proportionate, yet socialists and Democrats would never agree because such a system would eliminate their ability to use the tax system for social engineering and in particular the redistribution of wealth.

It is important here to address two common socialistic arguments against proportional taxation. First, socialists feel if all taxation were proportionate it would be impossible to fund all government services. This argument's flaw lies in what constitutes government services. It is right and legitimate that government provides certain essential services such as police, fire protection, roads and sewers. Indeed, this is one of government's core obligations and reasons for existence. Unfortunately, socialist ideology requires government to support people according to need through the redistribution of wealth, requiring massive spending and high taxes. If government were responsible for only the essential services then government would be able to better provide essential services with less money. The tax burden would be reduced, and there would be enough money for the essential services. The socialistic desire to redistribute wealth increases taxes, makes taxes non-proportional and makes it difficult for government to fulfill its proper role of providing essential services. Socialists fail to admit the government does not have the money for these essential services because so much is being spent on social engineering programs that redistribute wealth.

Secondly, socialists object that if taxation were based entirely on proportionality, some people literally could not afford to use the roads. It is important to realize this is more a practical argument than a moral one. It is practical because roads are more essential to society than equalizing wealth. It argues some people must pay more because everybody needs roads yet some cannot afford to pay. This is a fair enough point and one that demonstrates why taxes cannot be based entirely on the benefits-used philosophy of taxation. However, a better compromise would be a flat tax, which is both mildly progressive and closer to the benefits-used philosophy, but the socialists would never agree to it because it would be more difficult to redistribute wealth.

Thanks to the socialists and their socialist amendment to the Constitution, the American tax system today is a complex disaster. Taxes are too high, they are non-proportional, there is not enough money for essential services, the federal deficit is ballooning and the entire system is patently unjust to many citizens. The driving force behind this state of affairs is the plague.


## The Redistribution of Wealth

Socialistic doctrine requires wealth to be redistributed. The only way to provide according to need is to take property from some and give it to the needy others, so socialism must necessarily redistribute the wealth it takes.

Virtually all taxes contain some form of redistribution. Sales taxes, property taxes, corporate taxes, inheritance taxes, excise taxes and capital gains taxes all redistribute wealth to one degree or another. There is one tax, however, favored by the socialists because it is the most effective tool for achieving wealth redistribution. That tax is the progressive income tax and it is the most egregiously unjust and mean-spirited tax levied by the federal government. America today is engaged in a massive redistribution of wealth, and it is doing it through the progressive income tax.

It is only human nature to want something free—there is no downside and all upside to the recipient. The progressive income tax is the vanguard for the "let the other person pay" syndrome, which the socialists are especially adroit at exploiting. Many people will naturally vote for socialistic government methods of taxation that bring benefits to them that others must pay.

This is socialist greed at its worst and it is one of their most pharisaic qualities. They wrap themselves in the self-righteous mantle of compassion when their real motivation is to get something for nothing. This willingness to let others pay is a central force behind America's redistribution of wealth policies and in particular the progressive income tax.

**Progressive Taxation**

In *An Inquiry Into the Principles and Policy of the Government of the United States* Virginia farmer and Jeffersonian John Taylor wrote there were two threats to the natural economic order. He stated there are *two modes of invading private property; the first, by which the poor plunder the rich…sudden and violent; the second, by which the rich plunder the poor, slow and legal.* Modern democracies under pressure from socialism have made this obsolete. Today, the poor plunder the rich slowly and legally, and their vehicle is progressive taxation.

Progressive taxation taxes individuals' incomes on a graduated basis. It is not a flat tax or a tax based on benefits received. It is not a proportional tax. The tax abandons any concept of justice in taxation. This tax concept is based on the socialistic belief that the amount of taxes one pays should reflect one's ability to pay.

A flat tax would be the same tax rate on the income of all taxpayers. If the flat tax were 10 percent, then the taxpayer with a $10,000 income would pay $1,000 and the taxpayer with a $100,000 income would pay $10,000. A flat tax is a form of progressive tax because even though the higher income taxpayers use the same amount of government services as lower income taxpayers, they pay more in taxes. The flat tax holds some claim to fairness because the rate is at least the same for all taxpayers.

The progressive tax or graduated income tax on the other hand taxes income at increasingly higher rates. The taxpayer with a $10,000 income may pay 10 percent, or $1,000, and the taxpayer earning $100,000 may pay 30 percent, or $30,000! Socialists claim this is only fair and right because the higher income individual has the ability to pay a greater share.

Section II of the *Communist Manifesto* demands a *heavy progressive or graduated income tax,* and in *Toward a Democratic Left* socialist Michael Harrington wrote America should have *only a progressive income tax and no other.* Indeed, socialists take great pride in having brought progressive taxation to

America. Clearly, the progressive income tax is the socialist's weapon of choice because it redistributes wealth so effectively.

In his book *Let Us Talk of Many Things*, William F. Buckley asked why *a taxi driver who elects to work seventy hours a week should be taxed at a higher rate than a taxi driver who works forty per week.* A progressive tax is discriminatory because it penalizes those who work the hardest or have the talent to make the most. It is a tax that is intuitively wrong. The intuitive thing is to reward those who work the hardest and are the most able. Progressive taxation does the opposite — it penalizes effort and rewards indolence. The harder an individual works, the more he or she is penalized under socialism. Progressive taxation simply perpetrates injustice to some citizens.

Progressive taxation does not treat all citizens equally — it discriminates against one segment of the population. It makes the hardest workers subsidize others by declaring what they earn is not theirs to keep but rather belongs to the entire population. To justify this discrimination, socialists invoke the concepts of social justice and social equality. This commits an injustice to the individual in the name of justice for the collective group, which means collective justice is more important than individual justice. Socialism is an ideology that justifies perpetrating injustice to selected individuals. This socialistic injustice has been exclaimed by numerous unheralded, unnamed and rarely quoted individuals over the years such as J. R. McCulloch, who wrote the following:

> The moment you abandon the cardinal
> principle of exacting from all individuals
> the same proportion of their income or of
> their property, you are at sea without rud-
> der or compass, and there is no amount of
> injustice and folly you may not commit.

A. Thiers warned that *progression is simply hateful arbitrariness*; and John Stuart Mill described progressive taxation as a *mild form of robbery*. Socialist's support of progressive taxation is conspicuously hypocritical because they tout justice on one hand but commit injustice with the other — they support equality and non-discrimination in, for example, gender and race but not in taxation.

The socialists in their convoluted view of the world call this injustice to the individual justice. Socialists like Michael Harrington turn the concept of justice on its head. They claim the wealth accumulated by the able is unjust because it results in an unequal disparity of wealth. They believe any accumulation of wealth that is not used to provide for the poor according to need is injustice. They call this social justice, but social justice to whom? It is not social justice to discriminate unfairly against some individuals under progressive taxation. To those discriminated individuals it is a personal and real injustice. For something to be just it must be fair and equitable for all and not a few. Socialist justice is selective, not universal, which is not necessarily justice.

Socialists further attempt to warrant progressive taxation as social justice by appealing to the concept of ability to pay. They claim an individual who is able to pay should pay, however it does not morally follow that merely because one has the ability one should be compelled. Like the earlier example, forcing one to pay more because one has wealth and is more able to pay is the same as conscripting the strong man to hard labor jobs or the smart woman to actuarial jobs. It is not social justice or any justice at all to compel someone to use his or her ability or to rob Peter to pay Paul. It is not justice to Peter because he has been robbed and there is no justice dispensed to Paul because he did nothing to earn it. Merely because one has the ability does not create a moral imperative to use a special ability. No God-ordained law says socialists have the moral right to make an ought from an is. The socialist concept of ability to pay is totalitarian, arbitrary, unjust and immoral.

Edward W. Younkins of West Virginia's Jesuit University did a masterful job of debunking any socialist claim to the morality and justice of progressive taxation in his paper titled *Taxation and Justice*. He describes some of the purported reasons for progressive taxation and why they are wrong. One socialist theory of justice used to support progressive taxation imposes equality of sacrifice. Briefly, Younkins describes the idea as follows: as incomes increase the importance of each additional dollar decreases, so taxing higher incomes involves less sacrifice per dollar than obtaining the equivalent revenue at lower levels of the income scale. In short, it is right to take more from the wealthy because they value it less. This is ideologically driven sophistry. Who decides the wealthy value their money less? There is no objective method to measure whether one person obtains more or less value from an additional dollar of income compared to other individuals. A poor artist may value his $1,000 inheritance far less than the businessman who earned $100,000. Further, whether an individual values one's own wealth more or less than others is a personal matter. Neither the state nor other people, including socialists, have the right to decide for the individual how much one values his or her personal property. It is contemptible of the self-righteous, arrogant and intolerant socialist to usurp that right. The individual has the freedom to decide for oneself and not the socialist.

Other theories used to support progressive taxation are the doctrine of the desirability of economic equality and the utility theory. Some hold that heavier taxes on higher incomes are warranted by the belief that inequalities are immoral. These egalitarians want to pull the successful back into the pack via the progressive tax. But there is no God-ordained right to economic equality or to punish some people because they have more money. It would be like giving a slower runner a head start in order to equalize his chances of winning against the faster runner.

Socialists often appeal to the concept of utility to support progressive taxation. Generally, they say the tax is good because it is useful, it works and it promotes the greatest happiness. They claim any injustice perpetrated onto some under this rubric is justifiable because of the overall good it does. The problem is that the concept of utility is entirely subjective. One could value leisure (or the avoidance of effort) as utility and argue the opposite. More importantly, under totalitarian socialism it is the socialists who decide what utility means and not the individual. In other words the individual loses the freedom under the socialist's utility theory to decide for themselves the definition of utility or what makes them happy.

Younkins goes on to provide additional reasons, many of which have been discussed in this book, why progressive taxation is wrong. These include the loss of the individual's right to life, liberty and happiness; the destruction of incentive; the loss of citizen respect for the tax laws and a decreasing willingness to obey such laws; the dampening of the spirit of helpfulness and voluntary charity; and the pejorative effects of using taxation as an instrument for social change. Significantly, Younkins emphasizes socialism's violation of the rule of law when the poor majority votes a tax rate for the rich minority to which the majority themselves are not subject. This is not social justice but rather unjust tyranny of the majority. For any society to maintain the rule of law, all individuals must stand equally before the tax law and be subject to the same rate. It is wrong to assume the rights of the wealthy minority are any less than the needs and wants of the poor majority. Younkins states:

> [To the] founders of our country, welfare meant providing the necessary common conditions for people to fare well on their own by seeking their own happiness, prosperity, and success. They did not mean providing benefits to some particular group or locale.

It is clear that the progressive tax is an invitation to the majority to discriminate against a minority, and the socialist's pretense of "social justice" to justify it is sophistry. The progressive tax violates one principle on which a democracy rests: the majority should not be able to apply to the minority a rule that it does not apply to itself. It discriminates by introducing a distinction, which aims at shifting the burden from those who determine the rates onto others. This is what is happening in America today; perhaps the best example of it is Social Security. Social Security was described by Hayek as

> an instrument for the compulsory redistribution of income. The ethics of such a system, in which it is not a majority of givers who determine what should be given to the unfortunate few, but a majority of takers who decide what they will take from a wealthier minority.

All laws must apply to those who lay them down and those who are subject to them equally—the governors should be treated the same as the governed. The rule of law demands this.

It should be mentioned that some socialists and Democrats today endeavor to escape this dilemma by claiming that progressive taxation does apply to everyone. They claim that the person with a low income who votes for a high tax on those with a high income are also voting to tax themselves at the higher income if they should get one. They claim they are being treated equally under the law because the same circumstances apply to both, that is both are taxed at a lower rate when they have lower incomes and at higher rates when they have higher incomes. This is more sophistic reasoning for many reasons. First, many unendowed with low incomes may never get to high incomes. Second, many of those with high incomes have them because they have the ability or expend the effort to make the higher income. It is because that individual has the ability or makes the effort that they are discriminated against under progressive taxation. The low-income person may not have the ability or ambition. Third, some may choose a low paying job with the knowledge that they will most likely never achieve a high income. And fourth, many will most likely never have a high income like those with little ambition, brains or talent. The truth is that some have more ability than others, and when taxation is based on "from each his ability," it is those with ability who are being penalized.

Using the earlier example, this defense of the progressive tax is analogous to a majority of slow runners passing a rule that requires the starting blocks for fast runners to be moved back so they have farther to run. The slow runners' reason for such a rule is that the slower runners should have an opportunity to win the race. Their justification for the rule is that if and when they become fast runners their starting blocks will also be moved back. The truth is that only a few constitutionally have the talent and tenacity to be fast runners and most slow runners will always be slow runners. Consequently, the odds are that the rule the slow runners passed will never apply to them, only to the fast runners. Beyond this, the faster runners should win the race. If they have the talent and work ethic to be fast runners then they should be rewarded for their abilities. They should win the race. Further, if a slower runner has less ability but works harder to become a faster runner, they also should be rewarded with a win. Pulling the block back in this case penalizes effort. Clearly, claiming that all are subject to the same rules in progressive taxation, like running, is an empty justification.

In truth it turns out that the socialist claim to soak the rich with progressive taxation really soaks the average, middle class, working and providential Americans who shoulder the bulk of America's responsibilities. The people raising families without governmental assistance, the ones who must make the most money to fulfill their responsibilities, the hardest working mostly middle class individuals are the ones hit hardest by the progressive tax. The real solution for the American middle class is to redistribute the socialists from whence they came. Progressive taxation is driven by the socialist need to redistribute wealth, so if the plague is eliminated so is the pestilence of progressive taxation.

## Socialism Is Theft

Socialist Pierre-Joseph Proudhon had it wrong when he said property was theft; a far better case can be made that socialism is theft. Thievery is the taking or removing of personal property with the intent to deprive the original owner. This is precisely what taxation does and what socialistic progressive taxation does very well. Socialists use exactly the same reasoning for the redistribution of wealth that a thief uses when robbing someone. The thief thinks "I have no money (the poor), you have money (the rich), I need money for me, my family, or my friends (redistribute and equalize wealth), you can get along without some of your money (you are rich), so I will take some of your money by force (progressive taxation)." This is a remarkable example of parallel thinking between thieves and socialists, a fact socialists loathe admitting. It is the same as robbing a bank, stealing a car or robbing a person at gunpoint except thieves go to jail and socialists get elected. Socialists avoid jail by legalizing their theft; socialist ideology makes thievery legal.

Socialists claim they are not thieves; they claim taxpayers get benefits and services for what is paid in taxes. This is simply not the case with the socialistic policy of wealth redistribution through progressive taxation. As already noted, this policy detaches taxation from any concept of benefits received. The very nature of wealth redistribution is to redistribute wealth and not to provide a commensurate level of services for taxes paid. Further, benefits socialists claim to deliver are not voluntary. Under a free market system buyers can choose whether to pay for a benefit. They may not want the benefit because they do not want to pay for it. They may prefer to keep their money. Socialists offer no such choice; they tell the individual what benefits one is to pay for under threat of force.

In his book *History of Socialism* Harry W. Laidler referred to the socialist students of Vienna in the late 1800s who marched on behalf of the Austrian people who had long suffered under *cruel despotism where the laws were passed and taxes enacted without consultation of the people.* The socialistic majority today is enacting similar cruel and despotic laws that tax Americans without consulting many and especially the minority. These laws are being enacted to further the socialist goal of wealth redistribution through progressive taxation. Socialists are enacting arbitrary, capricious, unjust and coercive tax laws. They are taking Americans back to the very circumstances those Viennese students were protesting.

Clearly, any government that promulgates unjust laws will not survive long. The future consequences of this oppression and where these socialistic tax laws are taking America will be examined next.

## Increasing Lawlessness

Earlier you read the story of a Russian farmer who stopped working under socialism; he had lost his incentive to work because his neighbors took his crops. A more likely scenario is that he continues to work because he and his family need the harvests to survive but now does everything he can to hide it from his neighbors. He hides his fields, harvests at night and hides the crop. So the modern day individual under socialism often cheats on taxes, lies to the government and uses the black market.

As socialism grows in America more people will become dependent on governmental benefits and increasingly view benefits as entitlements. These dependent people will agitate for the preservation and expansion of their benefits. To satisfy this insatiable demand, the government must pass escalating taxes aimed at those citizens most able to pay. Consequently, American society will increasingly divide into two groups, those who pay taxes and those who do not: a taxpaying class and a non-taxpaying class. The paying class will increasingly resent the government and lose respect for the government and its tax laws. Their reaction will be predictable and all too human. They will think, "If the government is willing to commit an injustice to me then I have no moral obligation to obey its laws, so I am free to commit injustice to the government." They will endeavor to skirt the law to avoid paying taxes, and the inevitable result is lawlessness.

It is the beginning of the end. As society becomes less moral and more coercive, people lose respect for the government, cooperate less with the government, endeavor to avoid the government, evade taxes by hiding income and assets from the tax collector and avoid governmental systems and institutions. The most conspicuous manifestation of this degradation of society due to socialism is the growth of black markets. People will increasingly solicit and rely on illegal markets to meet needs and avoid the government. In the final phase of the failed communist Soviet Union, for example, it was estimated that 45 percent of their economy was "off the books." In Cuba, most food and supplies are obtained from the black market; Sweden has a huge black market for housing; and in Italy it is almost a religion to avoid paying taxes by hiding income from the government.

The government gets caught in a squeeze. On one hand, it collects fewer taxes because people are avoiding the system and the productive tax-paying class works less thus lowering their taxes; on the other hand, socialists are demanding more benefits. The government must become more coercive and totalitarian to make the taxpaying class pay more, but this only drives those citizens further underground. Civil disobedience commences, and the whole system begins a long spiral to destruction. This is what occurred in socialist Argentina. Argentina's system faltered because half of its population clamored to maintain benefits while the other half avoided the government. The result was their society and economy spiraled downward into lawless chaos.

There are a number of lessons to be learned from all of this. First, this is what happens when the law abandons morality, and in particular justice, as a premise. Socialistic redistribution of wealth through progressive taxation policies has no moral force because the policies are unjust to many citizens. Second, other laws within the society lose moral force because people will not oblige just laws if they are treated unjustly by other laws. The law cannot ask for obedience based on justice in one law and then commit injustice through another law. The government and its laws lose moral authority, hence citizens no longer feel obligated to obey. The government's right to ask for obedience to the law based on justice has been abrogated. Consequently, the law becomes increasingly based on "might makes right," and the result is lawlessness.

Third, socialists argue the redistribution of wealth eases social unrest; it placates the poor. In reality, the forced redistribution of wealth has the opposite effect. It not only increases social unrest but also hastens divisiveness, discord and a society's decline, which is happening in America today. This socialistic argument to redistribute wealth because any disparity of wealth causes social unrest supports the idea that the policy itself is not based on justice but rather on ostensible practical considerations.

Fourth, laws that make people lawbreakers are bad laws. If people avoid paying taxes due to unjust socialistic tax laws society ends up with a great many guilty people. Are the people really guilty or are the laws that made them guilty bad laws? In the case of progressive taxation, the answer is clearly the law is at fault. Fifth, the mere revelation that the government is squeezed under socialism demonstrates that socialism fails at producing wealth and exists only as a parasite on other systems. The parasitized system in America is capitalism. The non-taxpaying beneficiaries under socialism must squeeze more because the pie is getting smaller. The pie is getting smaller because the entrepreneurial wealth producers are working less and not cooperating with the government. Socialistic governments must squeeze the productive capitalist side more like a parasite slowly killing its host to placate the socialist side. This is what is happening in America today.

Let us now focus on the totalitarian nature of socialism.

# Totalitarianism

Recall earlier contemporary socialist Michael Harrington was quoted saying that socialists must focus on influencing the federal government in Washington, D.C. as the only way to institute a socialistic agenda—local governments must be forced to conform to a national socialist doctrine. This kind of thinking is what makes socialism a naturally totalitarian political philosophy. Socialism mandates the state control of the means of production and distribution of wealth. Having the state control production requires considerable state power and influence. It must have the capacity to own and control all of the services and industries within the state. With these industries the state must manage the degree, extent and capacity of production. When the state controls the distribution of wealth it must identify the wealth, confiscate it and distribute it.

Under socialism the state and not the market becomes the arbiter of production and distribution. It decides what to produce, who gets it and how much they get. Socialism also requires each citizen to produce according to ability and receive benefits according to need. Because some are more able than others, socialism will naturally require some to produce more than others, for which it offers no reward. Consequently, it must increasingly "boot and spur" its most productive citizens so they will work according to their ability and care for others less able.

None of this philosophy squares with reality. People naturally prefer to control their own production to distribute or keep their own wealth and resist coercion, so for the socialistic state to work it must force compliance. The state must become more totalitarian under socialism to make socialism work. Worse, when the state controls wealth private property is destabilized, and in extreme socialistic states there is no private property. All of these add up to bigger and more totalitarian government.

F. A. Hayek explains the socialistic economic necessity to become totalitarian as

> the need for organization and central planning. He wrote that inherent in socialism is the belief that scientific ideals should be applied to the problems of society. This application occurs through organization and central planning, which must necessarily be forcibly imposed.

He quotes a German socialist, Johann Plenge, who said *it is high time to recognize the fact that socialism must be a power policy, because it is to be organization...socialism has to win power.*

Hayek expanded on this theme in *The Constitution of Liberty*. Ignorance is a condition of freedom because if man were omniscient there would be little case for liberty. Man would have perfect knowledge and therefore the perfect form of government. But man is not perfect or omniscient; therefore, liberty is essential in order to leave room for the unforeseeable and unpredictable. It is because we each know so little and which of us knows best that we trust the independent and competitive efforts of many to induce the emergence of what we want when we see it. He continued the advance and even preservation of civilization are dependent upon a maximum of opportunity for accidents to happen.

The consequence of this *involves risks deliberately taken, the possible misfortune of individuals and groups who are as meritorious as others who prosper, the possibility of serious failure or relapse even of the majority.*

Essentially, all institutions of freedom are adaptations of ignorance, circumstances that deal with chances and probabilities and not certainties. Hayek continues:

From this foundation of the argument for liberty it follows that we shall not achieve its ends if we confine liberty to the particular instances where we know it will do good. Freedom granted only when it is known beforehand that its effects will be beneficial is not freedom.

For Hayek this freedom of ignorance is most conspicuously manifest in any societies respect for the freedom of speech. John Stuart Mill presaged Hayek when he wrote *the strongest foundation for any belief is a standing invitation to prove it unfounded.* Both Hayek and Mill are expressing the public discourse theory: truth is produced when conflicting ideas collide, a process which makes error and untruth conspicuous.

Under utopian socialism this freedom of public discourse is discouraged or eliminated. Sweden's smothering social norms, Cuba and Russia's censure of dissidents and the admonition for political correctness in America are just a few examples. It is in the nature of socialism and utopian thinking to suppress discord and opposing views because many utopians believe human ignorance is diminishing as scientific knowledge advances. It is because of this scientific advancement in knowledge that the socialists believe the deliberate control of all human activities through rational central planning is desirable. The result is that socialistic totalitarianism, and lack of tolerance ultimately suppress a society's progress. Socialistic utopias freeze humans and hinder their advancement because they limit the freedom to fail, disagree, think independently and do things differently. In their zeal to eliminate the *misfortune of individuals and groups* they are collaterally hindering human development.

Under socialism the individual is forced to work, forced to give up the fruits of personal labors, deprived of private property and forced to provide for others according to need. And it is under socialism that the individual is vilified and sometimes jailed if they resist. People find themselves living in a state that is increasingly and necessarily despotic, tyrannical and oppressive: a socialistic totalitarian state.

The word procrustean comes from the Greek mythological legend of Procrustes. Procrustes was a giant of Attica and a robber who captured wayfarers and placed them on his iron bed. If they were longer than the bed he amputated overhanging limbs. If they were shorter he stretched them until they fit the bed. So, attempt to reduce all people to a standard belief or pattern of behavior is known as placing them on Procrustes's bed. Procrustean philosophies are intent on promoting conformity at any cost, sometimes arbitrarily and sometimes violently. Socialism is a procrustean philosophy that forces people onto its political ideological iron bed. The philosophy does not account for human nature. People naturally want to acquire property and keep what they have earned. So again the state must become increasingly coercive for socialism to succeed, which makes socialism an inflexible ideology and not a flexible political doctrine. It is an ideology that claims exclusive truth unlike a political doctrine that involves compromise. The best political doctrines and politics themselves are protean and changeable, which allows them to accommodate people's natural inclinations.

Socialism is an inflexible and intolerant ideology that labels alternative political doctrines as false ideas. Socialism's aim is to *abolish politics and create a perfect society via social engineering*. The famous British political philosopher Edmund Burke abhorred such philosophies. He believed people should be ruled by their temperament and not by an ideology. He was a pragmatist, not an ideologue, who advocated flexible government to avoid the totalitarian consequences that arise under socialism.

Socialism's unrealistic ideology is founded on the idea that human beings are of value only as members of a collective group and not as individuals. People's worth is defined by how well they fit in and contribute to the group. Analogously, in socialism people are like ants in an ant colony.

The colony is all-important, and the individual ants exist to support it. Each ant is a small, insignificant robotic cog in an impersonal machine. Individual ants are not allowed to keep what they have produced and are doomed to living a life within a totalitarian colony at the same social and material station throughout their lives. There is no individuality, individual free expression or individual freedom. Their life is to be born, to live as laborers and then to die. Problematically for socialism, humans are not ants. Indeed, as the world's leading authority on ants, E. O. Wilson once wrote about socialism: *good theory, wrong species*. Human beings have souls and think, and their spirit eschews living under gray norms superintended by an oppressive, authoritative and totalitarian socialistic government. Individuals do not like to be dragooned into living preordained lives.

History demonstrates the totalitarian nature of socialism. All socialistic states are or have been totalitarian to one degree or another. The former Soviet Union murdered and incarcerated people, engaged in forced relocations, had limited travel rights, took property without due process, limited religion and tried to control thought through propaganda and manipulation of the news. Indeed, it is within the doctrines of Karl Marx and Nikolai Lenin that socialism is to be achieved by violent force and maintained through constant revolution. Socialist Joseph Stalin took these policies to heart and killed millions. In Cuba, Fidel Castro shot and incarcerated dissenters, took people's property and limited freedom of travel. Similar totalitarian acts are found in the socialistic states of China, North Korea and Vietnam. Indeed, the forced relocations in many of these socialistic countries are mandated by the *Communist Manifesto* where, in Section II, it decrees the distribution of the population between the cities and country. People cannot choose where they want to live under these extreme forms of socialism. In Sweden and France, totalitarianism mostly comes in the form of coercive laws, stifling societal shame, disapprobation and ridicule to achieve political correctness. The term political correctness so commonly used in America today that it is, depending on its context, a euphemism for socialism. To be politically correct often means to adopt the doctrines of socialism.

The greatest threat of socialistic totalitarianism is to individual freedom. Indeed, in 1944 Austrian economist Hayek wrote *The Road to Serfdom* in which he maintained that freedom is impossible in a planned socialistic economy. Socialists know this so they endeavor to alter the concept of freedom by reorganizing reality. For example, British socialist economist Barbara Wootton responded with the idea that *a planned society can be a far freer society because justice is the parent of freedom.* This is a socialist convolution of the very concept of freedom. Granted, the justice that restrains people from harming one another does promote freedom, but this is very different from Wootton's socialist justice where society is planned to redistribute wealth. "To each his need" may provide security for some but to do so it must commit injustice to others. Freedom cannot be derived from this form of socialistic justice. To be just it must be just for all; if it is not, it is not justice. Her justice is not the parent of freedom but rather the adulterous parent to a bastard child; Hayek was right.

Socialists can always point to Marx's famous idea that under communism the state withers away so there can be no totalitarianism. History tells otherwise with the stubborn fact that under socialism and communism the state does not wither away but rather grows bigger, more menacing and increasingly totalitarian.

It is important to understand that some socialists can be dangerous people because they will do anything to bring socialism about even if totalitarianism is one consequence. Paul Johnson described this point poignantly in his book *Intellectuals*. He cautioned a wariness of utopian thinkers and especially socialistic utopian thinkers like Marx. Johnson wrote that utopian intellectuals are more interested in ideas than people. They are so preoccupied with creating the perfect society through social engineering that they ignore the individuals in society and often do them harm. The socialist's utopian orthodoxies generate irrational and destructive courses of action, which result in the *worst of all despotisms [and] the heartless tyranny of ideas.*

Johnson draws an important association between utopian socialist intellectual thinkers like Marx and violence. He describes Marx's appetite for power and taste for violence. Marx did not reject violence, or even terrorism, when it suited his tactics. Indeed, Johnson says if Marx had ever established himself in power it seems certain he would have been capable of great violence and cruelty. In due course socialist/communists Lenin, Stalin and Mao Tse-tung did practice on an enormous scale the violence Marx felt in his heart. Marx along with deterministic and anti-individualistic Leo Tolstoy also hated democracy because it provided citizens the opportunity to thwart their socialistic totalitarian utopian schemes. Johnson describes these kinds of intellectuals as *intolerant and progressive self-righteous thinkers* (note that Johnson uses the word progressive in a pejorative way).

Johnson's book makes a general case against social engineering of any kind. Indeed, he wrote *social engineering has been the salient delusion and the greatest curse of the modern age* and singles out socialists for special disapprobation with the following comments:

> Social engineering is the creation of millenarian intellectuals who believe they can refashion the universe by the light of their unaided reason. It is the birthright of the totalitarian tradition. It was pioneered by Rousseau, systematized by Marx and institutionalized by Lenin...social engineering, or the Cultural Revolution as it is called, produced millions of corpses in Mao's China... [which was]...applied by illiberal or totalitarian governments...[in addition]... all schemes of social engineering have been originally the work of intellectuals... [further]...a group of Marxist intellectuals, educated in Sartre's Paris, but now in charge of a formidable army, conducted an experiment [in Cambodia] in social engineering ruthless even by the standards of Stalin or Mao.

Johnson is saying something very important: Beware of all American socialistic intellectual utopian thinkers and their supporters. They carry the seeds of intolerance, totalitarianism and violence. To these ideologues, ideas are more important than people. It is far better to live in an imperfect society than a perfect totalitarian state.

It is also important to understand the relationship between socialism's totalitarian nature and the cultural divide in America today. The socialist wing of the Democratic Party, like Michael Harrington and Bernie Sanders, emphasize the need to focus on the federal government because with control of it they can impose their socialistic philosophy onto others. Such as philosophy, coupled with the increasing size and power of the federal government, has made control of it the battleground between the left and right. Whoever controls it controls the other, and whoever loses control of it becomes subservient to the other, which makes them less free to make their own decisions, control their own fate, control their own communities and live the way they want. We see this today in education. Many educational matters are mandated by federal law such as busing students to better schools and the availability of free lunches. The local communities have little control of these matters. If an individual or community objects to these mandates, the answer is invariably "there is nothing you can do about it because it is federal law," which only intensifies the struggle to gain control of the federal government. Clearly, this battle is becoming increasingly vicious and desperate, which is driving the cultural divide in America today.

The promoters of these causes are like André Gide, who ignorantly advocated communism even though he had never seen it and changed his mind when he actually visited the Soviet Union and got a taste of what true extreme socialism is like. Most of these socialist advocates have never lived in a socialistic state, yet they agitate for socialistic reform. They become increasingly intolerant with time and more willing to vilify any opposition to their socialistic ideology. They are simply dangerously ignorant of the long-term consequences of their beliefs. They are the ideologues that George Orwell was referring to when he wrote that *it is frightful that people who are so ignorant should have such influence.*

## The Loss of Wealth

Of all the arguments against socialism, the loss of wealth must be the most convincing. Even if one were willing to accept its other pejorative consequences including the loss of freedom, the loss of individuality, injustice and totalitarianism, it is hard to accept poverty. The inescapable denouement of socialism is poverty. It is the logical conclusion to a series of mistaken and misguided socialistic beliefs and actions that ultimately undo socialist states. There are real life-threatening consequences to some socialist ideas.

Virtually every socialist commune failed due to lack of wealth. Every socialist country mentioned in this book went bankrupt or is going bankrupt. The former Soviet Union went broke, Cuba and Argentina are broke and Sweden is struggling, not to mention the numerous other socialist countries in the world like North Korea and Venezuela that are struggling mightily against the rising tides of higher spending, higher debt, inflation, less productivity and the consequent loss of wealth. Even though America's federal deficit today exceeds $22 trillion[MR2] , mostly due to socialism, for now it does not have the problems other socialistic countries face because it is wealthy due to its capitalistic heritage. However, things are gradually and inevitably changing for the worse.

There are many reasons why socialism destroys a country's wealth. By destabilizing or prohibiting private property socialism removes the rewards, which attenuates effort and incentive. By providing according to need without condition, socialism creates dependence, which in turn causes higher government spending, higher governmental debt and higher taxes that further discourage effort and incentive. Socialistic governments initiate redistribution of wealth tax policies, so the rich pay for their programs, which only discourages effort and incentive further. With more in need, more people become consumers who are increasingly dependent on fewer producers. When they cannot generate enough income through taxes, socialists invariably turn to borrowing, which initiates a long spiral into debt and potential bankruptcy, further eroding a country's wealth. It is a wildly impractical and ideologically driven socialistic economic philosophy that gradually destroys the wealth of a nation.

Mentioned earlier, socialist governments rarely produce wealth. They concentrate on distribution and not production because they are incapable of wealth production. Government produces nothing; it can only regulate and distribute what wealth a country produces. Socialists try to produce wealth through central economic planning, but the attempts invariably fail. Stalin arbitrarily ordering more Russian tractors thinking they will bring prosperity simply does not work. The government ends up desperately prodding the socialist donkey rather than restraining the capitalist racehorse. The socialist state is caught in a dilemma: it wants the jobs but not that which produces jobs. These socialists do not understand the way to create wealth is to leave people alone, which is something they seem incapable of doing. Consequently, socialistic government must cannibalize its country's pre-existing wealth, which often was created by capitalism, to survive.

Socialistic governments can be compared to a company that manufactures and distributes a product. If that company neglects its manufacturing (or discourages it) and focuses only on distribution, the odds are it will fail in time. The company will find itself with an empty warehouse and nothing to distribute. Socialistic governments have excellent distribution capabilities but find themselves having less and less to distribute. To carry this analogy one step further, the company may decide it needs to build a new manufacturing plant to increase production, but if nobody works in the plant, the new facility will not solve the company's problem. Similarly, governments may build roads and bridges, but if nobody uses them they are worthless. Infrastructure, such as roads and bridges, may enhance wealth production, but it does not create wealth in and of itself, enterprising people in a competitive growing economy do.

There are numerous other reasons why socialism destroys wealth. Perhaps the most obvious is because people just stop working as hard. When needs are met without regard to effort, there is no need to work hard or perhaps at all. Another reason is the destruction of commercial markets. As Adam Smith predicted, socialistic governments become monopolies that work outside market forces, which destroys competition and ultimately markets. Socialistic governments also often nationalize industries, which then become less efficient monopolies, and prices go up for the consumer (the opposite consequence intended), whose purchasing power declines. The government must then increase taxes to subsidize these inefficient monopolies, which further discourages production. The destruction of legal markets by monopolistic socialistic government also gives rise to black markets to which an increasing number of people turn due to scarcity and avoidance of high sales taxes.

Smith also wrote that saving is discouraged under socialism because needs are provided. People stop saving because there is no need. With less saving there is less capital available for businesses to buy machinery and equipment that could be used to manufacture goods, so wealth growth is further discouraged. Socialism thus falls into a vicious downward spiral of wealth destruction. High government spending for benefits causes higher taxes and debt, which discourages production, which reduces revenue to the government. The consequence is relentless and continuing loss of wealth.

There is one specious socialist argument for government spending that should be addressed. Socialists say government distribution enables the economy to grow because people will then have the money to consume the products created within a private-market system. Unfortunately, this is a circular argument based on a false premise. As Ludwig von Mises and Murray Rothbard have pointed out, individuals cannot gain wealth unless they produce goods. Even if a people have money, wealth cannot be created if there is nothing to buy. Socialistic wealth transfer inhibits economic growth because it penalizes entrepreneurs for being successful, so less is available for purchase. The false assumption is that people can get money to spend without the creation of wealth. The socialist's argument is based on getting money to get wealth, but without wealth, the money to get it is worthless. Hence, their circular argument fails.

Free enterprise is a natural process that culminates in wealth. It begins with property ownership and the reward of keeping the fruits of one's labors. With reward comes incentive and more effort and inevitable competition, which fuels the process. It is a tightly woven and natural system where each part complements the others. The result is tremendous wealth and prosperity. Socialism does the opposite. With the state ownership of property, there are no rewards, which causes disincentive that brings indolence. With no competition, monopolies arise, enterprise is discouraged and wealth declines.

Socialism attacks every stage of natural wealth creation. Indeed, famous economist John Maynard Keynes wrote that socialism dampens enterprise. When socialism takes property, it removes enterprise and the dynamics between reward, incentive, effort and competition; the loss of wealth is the result.

The highest manifestation of this loss of wealth in America could be the recent towering foreign trade deficits. Trade deficits indicate many things including relative competitiveness, balance of trade payments and the trend of foreign indebtedness. They are also very much a measure of America's wealth, and indications are this wealth is dissipating. America's annual trade deficits are at all-time historic highs. In the early 1980s the annual trade deficits reached unprecedented levels. They peaked at a record $153 billion in fiscal year 1987, then shrank to a low of $31 billion in 1991 but grew again to more than $100 billion a year since 1994, reaching $113.7 billion in 1997. It seems obvious that America today is losing wealth.

Comparing socialism to a parasite may sound like hyperbole and excessive posturing; however, one cannot escape the many similarities between the two. Socialism, like a parasite, cannot exist on its own. Every extreme socialistic country mentioned in this book either has been or is in the process of eating away at its capital base. Socialism must have a host from which to feed to survive. It attacks and destroys the most capable and able producers within society, or the healthiest cells. It produces no wealth itself; it can only cannibalize other systems' wealth. When not infecting a host, it lays dormant, awaiting opportunity. Its favorite target is wealthy hosts, the ones that have the most blood to suck.

Conservatives, capitalists and businesspeople are the doctors trying to debride the parasite from the soma and return the patient to health, but the parasite is too resistant and usually fatal.

America today is fighting this parasite. It is struggling like an infected sick patient endeavoring to throw off an illness. Sadly, America is losing the war to the parasite socialism, which is not only draining its wealth but also slowly killing the American Dream.

## The Debt and Inflation

There are numerous ways socialism dissipates wealth. Principle among them is debt and inflation that plague virtually every socialistic society. Debt and inflation existed in the former Soviet Union, in France during the early 1980s and in Sweden and Cuba today. Argentina is drowning in debt and experiencing hyperinflation. The policies of socialism inexorably cause debt and inflation in economic systems. To justify this economic reality, socialists claim an *artificial separation of economics and politics* exists: they argue economics should not control politics but rather politics should dominate economics. They claim humans should be political and not economic. They claim the *economic man is dead*. Because this claim is so detached from reality, it is hard to address. The claim ignores scarcity, population, effort and a host of other inescapable realities of the human condition. One might as well say the cost of a gallon of gasoline will be $2.00 when in reality no gasoline will exist to be purchased; it is a meaningless gesture because there is no gasoline. Humans are necessarily subject to economics by the very nature of their existence.

Debt and inflation are inexorably connected due to the numerous socialistic policies that cause them. Some of these policies include full employment, minimum wages, excessive benefits and reduced working hours. Some of the consequences include loss of production, inefficiency and non-competitiveness. These circumstances are usually caused by socialistic governments that endeavor to provide goods and services according to need and spend beyond society's means.

Governments are confronted then with three ways to balance their budgets: cut spending, increase taxes or borrow money. Socialistic countries never reduce spending and already tax to the limit; they therefore must borrow. These countries invariably incur massive debt to pay for socialism's goods and services. When the government cannot repay the debt it prints money, which floods the economy with currency that devalues. Citizens are then faced with holding worthless money and paying for things that now cost more. Goods and services become more expensive, and savings are wiped out. At some point the choices are then to either raise taxes to cover the debt or reduce spending. Socialistic governments invariably do the former and rarely the latter. Taxes in socialistic countries are confiscatory, so socialist states necessarily reach a point where taxes cannot be raised any higher, so more debt is incurred. These are the circumstances America has been experiencing in the recent past. America has embarked on a program of increased government spending, due mostly to socialism, and increasing debt; the result has been inflation. Indeed, in the 1960s New York City *had borrowed heavily for expanded social welfare programs [and by] late 1974, city paper saturated the markets, driving up interest rates and causing steep losses.* It was only bailed out by President Ford who had *Congress approve a $2.3 billion line of credit for the city.* In this case it was a matter of the fox, the federal government, guarding the henhouse, New York City. America, like most socialistic countries, refuses to reduce spending or live within its means. The defeat of many efforts to bring a balanced budget amendment to the Constitution is evidence of such fiscal irresponsibility.

Consider the average American's change in attitude toward debt under the influence of socialism. Americans abhorred debt in the past. Two hundred years ago Benjamin Franklin admonished Americans to *neither a borrower or debtor be.* Historically, Americans often saved to buy a car or house. They would not buy something until they could afford it. This ethic has been weakened by socialism, and today instant gratification through debt accumulation is the norm. Americans currently carry the highest individual debt in history through credit cards, mortgages, second mortgages, consumer loans, home equity loans and car loans; they are drowning in debt. Collaterally, Americans' attitudes toward default and bankruptcy have also changed dramatically. Not so long ago bankruptcy carried a heavy negative social stigma; it was a dishonorable course to follow. It was unthinkable, even shameful to consciously walk away from an obligation, so people endeavored to do what they had promised. Today, people declare bankruptcy with aplomb. It is "no big deal" to run up debt and then walk away from it through a Chapter 11 bankruptcy. More Americans are declaring bankruptcy today than ever in history. Socialism, which teaches all should have according to need, ignores its own debts to provide goods and services. When the socialist government finds it cannot repay that debt, it declares bankruptcy by devaluing its currency. Why should one expect any such country's citizens to act otherwise? If the government is not fiscally responsible, why should its citizens be? Socialism teaches the wrong lessons.

As time passes, economic matters typically deteriorate in socialistic countries. Fueled by debt economics and costly socialistic programs, the standard of living temporarily increases, but production slows, which increases the cost of goods and services relative to other non-socialistic countries. The socialist country then starts losing wealth. The nineteenth-century Irish banker Richard Cantillon explained this phenomenon:

> When the excessive abundance of money…
> has diminished the inhabitants of a State,
> accustomed those who remain to a too
> large expenditure, raised the produce of the
> land and labour of workmen to excessive
> prices, ruined the manufactures of the state
> by use of foreign productions…the money
> produced…will necessarily go abroad to
> pay for imports; this will gradually impov-
> erish the State and render it in some sort

dependent on the Foreigner, to whom it is obliged to spend money every year...[and] poverty and misery follow.

[The State]...will inevitably fall into poverty by the ordinary course of things. The too great abundance of money, which so long as it lasts forms the power of State, draws them back imperceptibly but naturally into poverty.

This is what is occurring in America today. Socialistic federal government policies have *raised the produce of the land and labour of workmen to excessive prices,* so America's manufacturing base is fleeing overseas. Mexico and China manufacture many goods Americans consume today. Consequently, the country's principle source of wealth, manufacturing, is fading, and jobs with it, and the trade deficit is at an all-time historic high. America is sliding into inevitable socialistic poverty.

The relationship between inflation and socialism is more complex. Lenin said the best way to destroy the capitalist system was to debauch its currency; doing so would cause inflation, which would allow the government to secretly confiscate the wealth of its citizens without observation. Lenin was correct, but what he failed to mention was that inflation also debauches the currency in the socialist state. Either way, it destroys wealth.

Inflation is essentially about supply and demand. It occurs when too much money is chasing too few goods, a situation caused by either an increase in the money supply or a decrease in the amount of goods. Socialism causes inflation both ways: by increasing the money supply and thus demand and by decreasing the amount of goods with lower production. By tampering with the free market to make economics conform to politics, socialism prints money, increases demand and decreases supply. The result is inflation.

Socialism increases demand many ways including requiring full employment, higher wages, minimum wages, make-work legislation and massive government benefits and entitlements. It decreases supply by discouraging profits and incentive, increasing the cost of production through higher wages and benefits, mandating shorter working hours, decreasing efficiency, curtailing private capital and investment and discouraging innovation, which preserves obsolete industries. It exacerbates the problem when it attempts to cover debt by printing money and borrowing from foreign countries. The last problem is common among socialistic countries. The French socialists during the early 1980s complained their economic problems were due to foreign countries like America; it was "impossible" for France to become a healthy socialistic country economically as long as America was capitalistic. They were in reality admitting France could not compete with America. Under socialism, France found itself producing less while its foreign neighbors were producing more. French goods were therefore expensive and foreign goods relatively cheap. Foreigners like Americans could purchase French goods for less than the average Frenchman, which drove up the prices of those goods for the French and caused inflation. Predictably, France suffered from high foreign debt and a high trade deficit because it was borrowing money from foreigners to make up the difference in purchasing power. This is the same problem played out in socialist countries like Sweden, and it is increasingly a problem in America.

Hayek addressed this problem of inflation and the welfare state. He explained that when governments control monetary policy the chief consequence is inflation and currency devaluation. The heavy financial burdens on socialistic welfare states can be temporarily alleviated by devaluing their currency. They simply print more money in order to pay back the debt causing inflation. Inflation, in short, lightens their load, but the problem is they are collaterally devaluing the citizens' money. They, as Lenin predicted, are debauching the fruits of their own citizens' labors.

## Business, Corporations and Socialism

Perhaps the best example of the loss of wealth in socialistic countries is the loss of businesses and business enterprise. In many ways business is the highest manifestation of capitalism because it is business that usually owns and manages the means of production and distribution of wealth. For socialism to succeed, the socialist state must wrest away that ownership from private enterprise. This struggle for ownership is most conspicuous at the business level and businesspeople are the front lines as capitalism's foot soldiers. Socialists have historically attacked the entrepreneur businessperson. Charles Fourier derided traders because they were superfluous and free enterprise because *there were too many merchants doing the same thing*. The intellectuals may wage the ideological battle between capitalism and socialism but it is fought at the businessperson's front door.

Compare the role and stature of the merchant in new, growing and struggling countries versus older, static established ones. The new country requires vital citizens engaged in commercial enterprises to create wealth. Consequently, it honors them and places them in positions of leadership. Early America respected and emulated its entrepreneurs. Andrew Carnegie, Henry Ford and Harvey Firestone were revered. They were among the entrepreneurs who made America wealthy. Once a society gains wealth and position, it takes the wealth these individuals created for granted and begins to think it does not need them anymore. The citizens' attitude under the auspices of socialism changes from awe of the entrepreneurs' accomplishments to desire to usurp the merchants' wealth. Socialism, which is common in older, established and wealthy nations, commences to degrade people of commerce. The process begins with restrictions on the forms of enterprise and progresses to confiscation of merchant wealth. Eventually, as in America today it vilifies the businessperson as greedy and selfish. Its final disastrous solution is to nationalize private businesses and just take wealth. The degree of the socialistic decline in any society in many ways can be measured by the stature of its merchants. Societies that honor them are ascending; those that dishonor them are on the decline.

Corporations are the primary targets of the socialists in America today, and socialists have developed a special hatred for them. They are the objects of their constant screed, venom and vilification. They are personified as the devil incarnate and labeled corrupt, dishonest and greedy. Socialists, in their zeal to defile corporations, even call them welfare recipients. These are misguided objections because businesses and corporations, not government, create wealth. Few countries are capable of creating wealth without some form of business enterprise.

Think of what the socialists are attacking. American corporations provide reasonably priced essentials such as food, housing and transportation; create jobs; and pay taxes. Because of the free market system they must serve citizens' needs efficiently and responsively or die. They exist only by meeting consumer demands within the framework of a competitive environment. They pay dividends to millions of people who have invested in them and rely on them for income. Most corporations are comprised of good, productive and hardworking people who are socially and environmentally conscious. They are some of America's most enterprising and able citizens. These people make this country's services and means of production function and support many charitable organizations. These corporations are also very democratic in nature because they are owned by and responsible to millions of shareholders from all strata of American society. Socialists, who berate these corporations live in the houses corporations build, eat the food corporations provide, drive the cars corporations produce and use the gas corporations distribute.

For these benefits, socialists deride corporations as welfare recipients. They complain about corporate welfare, a phrase that challenges one's ability to twist logic. It is not welfare when a corporation pays $1 million in taxes and then gets a $100,000 credit to hire minorities or buy certain machinery. It is a credit. Welfare is when one pays no taxes and receives something from the government for nothing. The twisted socialistic logic says "what you make is mine, so when I give it back to you, you are receiving welfare from me." How much stranger can it get?

Further, socialists hinder the corporation's ability to produce and distribute at virtually every step. They tax them with corporate, property and dividend taxes. They require them to withhold employee taxes and pay quarterly; to keep records and report employee income; to be licensed; to meet zoning restrictions; to meet occupational and health standards; to comply with the American Disabilities Act; to meet building code requirements; to meet environmental standards; to pay a minimum wage; to deal with unions; sometimes to give notice before a plant closure; to meet antidiscrimination policies in race and gender; to insure employees do not sexually harass one another; to provide paid family leave; to not fire anyone indiscriminately (such as for age); to produce safe products (or face class action suits); to meet Securities and Exchange reporting requirements (or face criminal sanctions); and to pay governmental fees, among a slew of other regulations and requirements. Certainly there are legitimate reasons to regulate corporations. Everyone would agree that children should be protected, the environment should not be fouled, products should be safe and everyone should be honest. These are laws that enhance not only society but also capitalistic competition. Many of these laws are compatible with capitalism and free enterprise. Unfortunately, socialism uses business regulation as a means to socially engineer and ultimately attain socialistic ends. Socialistic social engineering and regulating is diminishing American corporations, so it is a wonder anyone in America today would want to start a business enterprise because socialists make it so incredibly difficult.

Most socialists, including socialist politicians who are passing these anti-corporate and repressive laws, often have no clue what it takes to run a business. Most have never had the responsibility or dealt with the problems businesspeople face when juggling the various components of production and distribution. One simple and easy solution would be to require, like the military draft, all Americans to operate a business at one time or another in their lives. They should be required to deal with production, distribution, transportation, raw materials, bills, employees, unions, government regulation, lenders, debt, shareholders, taxes, uncertain markets, marketing, management, facilities, and wages — and to do it all without a loss. They should be required to operate a business as efficiently and cost effectively as today's corporate executives do. Americans may then come to better appreciate what challenges businesspeople and the corporations they manage face.

Socialists have developed a laundry list of empty and ideologically driven merchant evils, a few of which will be addressed here. They say merchants are greedy because they seek profits and chase money. Here socialists confuse greed with incentive; the profit motive, incentive and ambition are not necessarily greed. They claim that the merchant's goals of money and wealth are empty—they represent a "Willy Loman" emptiness of the American Dream. Seeking sustenance and security through the accumulation of money and creation of wealth are essentials for healthy individuals, and the proper handling of production is critical for any society's welfare. Business is based on competition and a healthy society should be based on cooperation. On the contrary, humans are naturally competitive, competition creates wealth, most socialist societies are monopolies and businesspeople cooperate all the time. Predictably, socialists claim the state should control the means of production and distribution of wealth, not private enterprise. There are endless counterarguments to this accusation, most of which are contained in this book, including that socialism destroys wealth, commits injustice, lessens freedom and is totalitarian and unrealistic. Most importantly, private enterprise produces better than most socialist states.

In the 1920s President Calvin Coolidge said *the chief business of the American people is business* because business brought prosperity. That prosperity and the American corporations that create it are the envy of the world. It is wealth made possible by the capitalistic system, a system proven superior to other failed socialist and communist ones. Most countries aspire to America's level of material success and high standard of living. Socialist countries cannot even begin to match America's success, yet socialists today only deride the businesses that helped bring it and wealth they have created.

## Intolerance of the Disparity of Wealth

A common theme in socialist literature is the evil of wealth disparity; the rich have too much and the poor have too little. The implication is that the rich have cornered the wealth, not created it and kept it from the poor. They have somehow usurped the wealth and denied the poor their rightful share. Socialists universally see injustice when some live in comfort and others in want; therefore, socialists vilify anything that smacks of wealth disparity.

First, there is nothing inherently wrong with being rich, and God did not ordain that everyone should have equal wealth. If God ordained anything it would be the unequal distribution of wealth because he made humans unequal; God must have intended them to have unequal capacities to acquire wealth. There is no universal and timeless moral that says it is wrong to be wealthy, so the socialists' desire for an equal distribution of wealth is a sentiment and not a moral imperative.

Further, accumulating wealth is not injustice. For something to be unjust, a wrong must be committed. A person must be unjustly or unfairly treated. There must be some damage. Able persons working to their ability endeavoring to succeed are merely doing what they do best and reaping the rewards. They do not inflict injustice on others. It is fanciful to claim that a poor person has been treated unjustly because another person has achieved wealth through personal effort. No moral stipulates a poor person is entitled to wealth; indeed, if there is a moral, it would have to be that individuals are entitled to the fruits of their labors. They are entitled to any wealth they have created.

More importantly, if one believes in freedom one must allow for a disparity in wealth—it is inherent in the definition of freedom that some are free to get rich. It comes with the territory. If people are denied the right to get rich they are denied freedom. The philosopher John Locke wrote that humans have a natural right to life, liberty and property. Indeed, it has been said that the sophistication of a society is determined by its willingness to tolerate the unequal distribution of wealth, which makes socialists unsophisticated.

Ask yourself a few questions about rich people. How did they get their wealth? Did they earn it or was it given to them? Was it because they worked hard or because customs, laws and circumstances worked in their favor? Would the wealth exist without the rich person? In other words, did they create the wealth? If they did, why ought they be derided? What are they doing with their wealth? Are they improving society or not? John D. Rockefeller, for example, used his wealth to virtually eliminate yellow fever from the globe, Andrew Carnegie built libraries and Bill Gates poured millions into cancer research. Alternatively, are they using their wealth to pamper themselves? Also, what constitutes a rich person? Is a person with $500,000 in assets who is providing for a family, paying for college and trying to save for retirement rich? There are different reasons for being rich, different characteristics of the rich and different consequences of wealth, none of which socialists seem to appreciate. Socialists lump the wealthy all together and call them despairingly "the rich." Effort and ability have much to do with the disparity of wealth, and not all rich people are bad.

Many rich people earned their wealth. They worked, took risks and often established business that created wealth. In the process they paid taxes, created jobs, produced products and services, and created wealth for the community. They have earned the right to be rich. They are an asset to society. Indeed, Saint-Simon's Utopia was managed by this group, who he called industrialists.

Unfortunately some rich were given wealth. It was achieved without effort, ability or risk. If there were a legitimate target group of rich deserving the socialists' disapprobation, this group would be it. Having achieved wealth without effort, ability or risk, they are often self-indulgent, idle and live in luxury. These truly are the non-productive idle rich. Many of the early Utopian socialists called this group the *spurring privileged few aristocrats*.

Capitalism and free enterprise offer the opportunity to get rich but do not guarantee it. Socialism vilifies the rich and does not offer the opportunity to get rich— it removes the opportunity. The former is a positive and optimistic philosophy, and the latter is a negative and pessimistic one.

Kevin Phillips in his book *Wealth and Democracy* derides the disparity of wealth in America — he is against all excessive wealth. However, he never distinguishes between Bill Gates, who made his fortune, and the Rockefeller heirs who inherited theirs. Who cares if Bill Gates has $85 billion — he made it himself. He created that wealth with his own efforts. His good fortune should be rejoiced because he was successful and created such tremendous benefits for not only himself but for society as well. Phillips' socialist derision of wealth does not account for a capitalist system that allows individuals the freedom to become wealthy. He decries a disparity that was created by a system that creates enough wealth so there can be a disparity. Without the system, there would be less wealth and no disparity. Put another way, socialistic countries do not have this disparity because they are usually poor, whereas capitalist countries do because they are usually rich. Would you rather live in a poor country where you and everyone else is poor or in a rich country with some rich people, more abundance and the opportunity to get rich yourself?

So, not all rich people are bad and some are very good, which is an observation Phillips and most socialists fail to appreciate. Further, socialist policies like progressive taxation and the redistribution of wealth penalize the rich and dampen ambition. By throwing the baby out with the bathwater, socialists turn the American dream of rags to riches from a virtue to a vice that ignores the benefits the rich provide.

# Socialism Oppresses

One often overlooked irony of socialism is, even though it claims to be the liberator of the oppressed, it also oppresses in many ways. At the top of the list is the able individual who has the will, ambition and attitude to make a large income and accumulate wealth. Socialists, who champion freedom from oppression, oppress this very individual. They oppress them because their philosophy requires those with ability pay. This translates to the imposition of oppressive progressive taxation—the more they make the greater the penalty with proportionately higher taxes. Certainly, oppression must include the 25 percent of America's top earners who are made to pay 84 percent of the federal income tax and the top 1 percent who are made to pay 37.4 percent. Socialists self-righteously demand freedom from oppression and then oppress.

Perhaps socialism's most sinister form of oppression is its totalitarian nature. History has demonstrated that under socialist totalitarian states people are subdued, directed, controlled and manipulated. Those who resist are often incarcerated, deported or shot. It is no coincidence that some of the worst atrocities against people, including gulags and pogroms, have been committed by oppressive socialist states and extreme communist ones.

Curiously, socialists claim people are physically oppressed if their needs are not cared for. Charles Fourier, for example, wrote of the drudgery and hunger caused by industrial England. Socialists' refer to societies like industrial England "holding" people in poverty. But industrial England did not cause hunger or poverty; they would have existed whether industrial England existed or not. Rather it afforded some the opportunity to get rich. It is not oppression when a person becomes wealthy through ability, it is rather opportunity. A better case could be made that industrial England helped alleviate hunger and poverty, created opportunity and elevated the average person.

This brings one to a very interesting and final form of socialist oppression. If oppression is the unjust, harsh or tyrannical exercise of authority then socialism must be its modern form. Socialism, with its collectivistic, wealth redistributing, totalitarian ways has replaced the historic forms of oppression to become the modern oppressor. In its zeal to make the individual responsible to the group, to be the arbiters of obligation and to force everyone to become their brother's keeper socialism has become oppressive. In its mild form it is an oppression that jails taxpayers if they do not pay unjustly higher progressive taxes, and in its extreme form it is often a tyrannical and despotic oppression that kills people like the kulaks of Russia for ideological purposes. Socialism is the oppressor of the able, the enterprising, the individual and the lover of freedom. It has become the predator. It has bastardized the very concepts of freedom and equality to gain power, which it often wields to oppress. It has become the greatest oppressor of all.

But it is worse than this because it is a personally degrading kind of oppression. In capitalism it is true impersonal forces may oppress a person. One may be, for example, laid off due to market forces. Under socialism this oppression becomes personal and degrading because it is caused by someone else. One is laid off not because of market forces but because some bureaucrat deemed it necessary. Hayek expressed this point clearly:

> Inequality is undoubtedly more readily borne, and affects the dignity of the person much less, if it is determined by impersonal forces than when it is due to design. In competitive society it is no slight to a person, no offense to his dignity, to be told by any particular firm that it has no need for his services or that it cannot offer him a better job.
>
> However bitter the experience, it would be very much worse in a planned society... [because]...his position in life must be assigned to him by somebody else.
>
> While people will submit to suffering which may hit anyone, they will not so easily submit to suffering which is the result of the decision of authority.

# Loss of Opportunity

The irony is that socialists believe they offer opportunity when in actually they deny it. They in particular deride the capitalistic system for lack of opportunity when that system offers far more opportunity than socialism itself.

Opportunity means in part creating the circumstances that offer opportunities. It means creating situations where there is opportunity to be had. Capitalistic America is the land of opportunity. America is rich, free and a place where a person literally can succeed through effort. Everyone wants to come to America because there is so much to gain. In America, an oppressed poor person can start a business, own property and get rich, opportunities that are denied or discouraged in socialistic countries. If a person hates a job or boss in America they can quit and work somewhere else or start a business and become an owner. Under monopolistic and totalitarian socialism people are told where to work, with whom and how much they are paid. They often cannot even own a business or property under socialism.

First, the un-endowed benefit from the able under capitalism. Many weak rely on the strong, and capitalism allows the strong to thrive. With that strength America today affords the weak the opportunity to live within a wealthy society created by those who are strong and enterprising. Ask yourself, how many opportunities do the weak have in the former Soviet Union or in Cuba today? Do people migrate to socialistic countries like Argentina, Sweden or even France for opportunities? They don't in part because those countries have few to offer.

Socialism, which claims to champion opportunity, limits it by diminishing freedom and choice. It blocks opportunity by taking the fruits of people's labors and oppresses with its totalitarian and inflexible government. Furthermore, it reduces people because it is incapable of producing the things they desire — it cannot produce the objects of opportunity. It cannot, for example, offer the opportunity to wealth because socialism cannot create wealth not to mention a car or house or apartment. Today, the parasite socialism lives off the opportunities in a healthy capitalistic body like America's and not a socialistic state's cadaver.

It is a uniquely pernicious form of lost opportunity. Inherent within the concept of opportunity is freedom of choice. Hayek addressed the consequence of this type of lost opportunity when he wrote the following:

> Nothing makes conditions more unbearable than the knowledge that no effort of ours can change them...[but the thought that]... we could escape if we only strove hard enough makes otherwise intolerable positions bearable.

## Divisiveness

There are many sources of divisiveness in any society, but socialism is one of the significant ones. Socialism brings divisiveness for six reasons. The first is that it makes people angry when government unfairly takes their property. The result is a permanent angry and resentful citizenry, festering irresolvable issues, black markets and often rebellion. John Locke in *Two Treatises of Government* wrote that any government that takes people's property is at war with the people, who then have no obligation to obey that government. He wrote:

> Whenever the Legislators endeavor to take away, and destroy the Property of the People, or to reduce them to Slavery under Arbitrary Power, they put themselves into a state of War with the People, who are thereupon absolved from any farther Obedience, and are left to the common Refuge, which God hath provided for all Men, against Force and Violence.

James Madison believed one of the primary purposes of government was to protect citizens' unequal faculties in acquiring property. With this historic insight, it should come as no surprise that contention and divisiveness are a natural result of socialism that institutes wealth redistribution. When productive citizens' property is taken, some citizens ardently resist and society divides.

Some consider disparity of wealth, the second reason, a divisive issue. Robert Reich, America's Secretary of Labor under President Bill Clinton, demonized the disparity of wealth in his book *Aftershock: the Next Economy and America's Future*. There are many reasons for wealth disparity, but one reason is due to unearned inheritance. Many thinking people accept rewarding talent and effort because it was earned. Most agree that Bill Gates is entitled to his wealth because he created Microsoft and the taxi driver in New York should keep his higher income because he works sixty hours a week compared to another's forty. Thinking people acknowledge that disparity of wealth is mostly due to unequal human ability and accept that. In this form, the disparity of wealth is not a divisive issue.

The problem is that socialism both wants equality of benefits and blurs the line between earned and inherited wealth. It no longer matters where wealth originated only that a disparity exists, and any disparity becomes an issue demagogues like Robert Reich dramatize beyond truth. Socialism makes the disparity of wealth a divisive issue.

The third divisive issue caused by socialism is unequal treatment under the law, and the best example could be inequitable taxation. Socialism in democracy instigates a tax-the-rich mentality that affects the most productive citizens. The result is resentment and ultimately divisiveness. Individuals who are targeted by their government to carry the burden of taxation usually respond with bursts of furious indignation and sometimes rebellion.

Consider the French Peasants' Rebellion in 1358 called the Jacquerie. The French nobility, merchant elite and clergy—privileged classes—had forced the peasantry to pay ever-increasing taxes, such as the hated *taille*, while they themselves held exemptions. The burden of taxes fell on one sect of the population and the result was the rebellion.

Fast forward to the year 2000 in mature democracy in America where a new group has been singled out to be treated unequally under the law in taxation. Now, 25 percent of American earners pay 84 percent of all federal income taxes while many Americans pay no taxes at all. The poor now are the privileged majority class exempt from taxation and able to pass the burden of taxes on to others.

Like the French medieval peasant, the American who earned their income also feels anger for being treated unequally under the law and targeted for higher taxation. Unequal treatment under the law, particularly in taxation, is a major source of divisiveness in late democracies.

The fourth reason is the concentration of power and imperious policies. Socialism does not come about naturally; it must be forced upon society. The violent phase did exactly that and failed, and the current Fabian phase is doing it gradually through the coercive power of government. Indeed, socialist Michael Harrington wrote that all economic planning should be centralized in Washington, D.C., which should impose its own priorities on local government—he of course means the federal government should forcibly impose socialism.

Many historic centralized powerful governments imposed single-minded imperious policies on all, and the consequences were multiple. In ancient Greece the oligarchs imposed their view on the people resulting in continuous internecine conflict. In ancient Rome the emperor imposed his views on taxation. In eighteenth-century France forced class stratification lead to inordinate taxation on the poor, which lead to the French Revolution. The American Revolution began largely in response to imperious tax laws imposed by England. Fast-forward two hundred years and the now powerful centralized American federal government is doing what all of these did earlier. It is an imperious government that is gradually imposing socialism that many Americans resist—this is a source of divisiveness.

The fifth reason is that socialism brings a relative free-floating morality and in particular utilitarianism or happiness for the most. Utilitarianism is a consequentialist moral theory that has no universal application. In it humans become the Protagorean measure of all things, which allows some, like the socialists, to commit injustice to others. It brings divisiveness because a socialist leader or the majority in democracy can be dictatorial, which often results in minority resentment.

Relative morality can also violate the rule of law and adherence to equal treatment under the law. Under relative morality an individual, such as a dictator or judge, could arbitrarily change the written law so what has been written is meaningless. They could also treat people differently under the law through socialism by making some pay higher taxes than others.

Relative morality's very definition is that morality is a social fact not grounded in any universal morality. This is a blank check for socialism that unleashes, legitimizes and enables it to enforce its opinion on all. Relative morality brings divisiveness.

The sixth and last reason socialism brings divisiveness is that demagogue politicians leverage it to gain power. This brings contention for many reasons, but the principle one is that it divides society into those who pay taxes and those who don't. Political power is often acquired by advocating an inflammatory issue — by fomenting contention rather than looking for common solutions. Contentiousness is a breeding ground for demagogues who seek power by pandering to the masses, advocating an issue they know is popular. Demagogic socialist politicians are particularly keen on inflaming the divide between the rich and poor. This is a source of socialist-driven divisiveness.

In the 1600s Louis XIV inflamed the French poor, pandering to the people's view that the rich were responsible for their evils. This, according to Tocqueville, inculcated revolutionary ideas that set the stage for socialism in France. It also caused divisiveness in French society that succored the French Revolution. Socialist demagogic politicians are doing the same in America today.

With socialism contention increases and factions become less tolerant, which makes compromise more difficult. These circumstances make for fewer statesmen looking for unifying common ground and more demagogues seeking to gain power by inflaming issues. The result is divisiveness due to the plague.


## General Philosophical Arguments

There exist many general arguments against socialism that do not fit elsewhere in this book. Some are oblique, philosophic and abstract. They are arguments that have been previously only touched on in this book and therefore explored incompletely. Many of these arguments are interrelated. This final section is a catchall for these arguments; a section of fragments. Philosophy is the love of wisdom, but what is wisdom? Certainly, wisdom can be measured in many ways, but clearly good judgment must be one of the components. One component of good judgment is the ability to discern what works and what does not work: the ability to do what succeeds in the end and the ability to choose a path or philosophy yielding positive consequences. Socialism is a philosophy that does not do this.

## Means vs. Ends

Socialists are willing to achieve social justice by any means, even if it involves committing injustice. Because their ends rarely occur naturally, they must sacrifice their ends to their means. They must sacrifice some utopian ends to the necessarily repugnant consequences of their means. Socialism too often must inhibit individuality, limit individual freedom, commit injustice, destroy wealth and become totalitarian to achieve its ideals. Indeed, one of the very reasons many do not support socialism is because of the dangers it poses to other values. Not only does socialism pose a danger to other values, but ironically also to some of the very values socialists themselves profess to champion. Therein lies one inherent contradiction in socialism; it often destroys the very things it desires. Its means often defeat its ends.

## Morality

Socialism's intellectual dishonesty is also the end of morality; socialism colors morals because they undermine one foundation of all morality, which is respect for the truth. Socialists often decide issues on relative merits, popularity or expediency without appeal to a moral code. The true meanings of words like justice become bastardized and often lose legitimacy. It becomes a free-floating concept word under socialism that does not exist in socialistic societies. This, along with Americans' inability to handle the wealth and freedom created by capitalism and democracy, is one reason America's moral code is being debauched. America is rapidly becoming a decadent society that indulges in unrestrained gratuitous sex and wanton violence. The moral codes are eroding, the moral compass is haywire and institutions that depend on morality, such as marriage, are being weakened. Socialism's intellectual dishonesty is one cause, as well as a symptom, of this decline.

## History

There exists a natural flow to human history. Things progress, change, evolve and adapt. It is like a free-flowing, wild and strong river constantly changing its course, creating sandbars and islands and altering the landscape. Some systems succor this free-flowing characteristic of human history and some impede it. The essential difference between these two forces is freedom. When a system is free, humanity is left unfettered to conceive and implement naturally occurring changes. If freedom is proscribed, humanity's ability to adapt is truncated. Free democracies and free markets are philosophies that succor this natural flow, and socialism is a philosophy that hinders it. It hinders the flow in many ways, two of which are significant.

Socialism hinders the development of humanity's political institutions. In a free democracy things may go right and things may go wrong, but one constant seems to be that things are always changing. However, democracies with freedom, like in nature, have a way of balancing themselves out in the end; they do not like disunity. The forces within the system are left free to counter any imbalances that may occur. Humanity adjusts with time, and history progresses.

Socialism is different. It subordinates freedom to security and therefore attenuates the give and take that succors change. It brings to fore the heavy, unyielding hand of government, and ultimately totalitarianism. Its political fixes are artificial, permanent, heavy and inflexible. It creates monolithic unalterable systems, such as Social Security, that take on a life of their own and create permanent barriers to change. Socialism's form of tampering works outside of nature and its fixes often become bigger than the original problem needing correction. Socialistic tampering is exacerbated as new fixes are added to "upgrade" old fixes. In the end, socialist manipulations create more problems than solutions because socialism has none of the elasticity inherent in the democratic system. It eventually develops an inertia that cannot be overcome and too many problems that cannot be resolved.

Economically, regulated free market capitalism harnesses human imagination and will, offers opportunities and allows for fluctuations in wealth. Such a system naturally flows and is vital, changing, enterprising and creative. Great innovations and advances have been made within this form of economic system. Socialism impedes this flow and is a system that freezes people into certain unchangeable obligations and duties. It freezes individuals economically. Socialism attenuates one's will and imagination and offers few opportunities. The heavy, centralized and bureaucratic socialistic hand of government is forever tampering with the economic flow of history to correct imbalances, but its tampering has consequences. When a socialist government increases wages with a minimum wage, for example, manufacturing decreases, unemployment goes up and society loses wealth. Similarly, when a socialist government offers more social services, it taxes progressively higher, causing the loss of incentive, which in turn causes less production and, again, the loss of wealth. In both cases, socialist tampering produces consequences opposed to the intended goal. Socialism impedes the natural flow of history like a series of dams on the once wild river. The dams have contained the river into a series of lazy, restrained, stagnant and sluggish lakes, which gradually kill fish runs.

## Mediocrity

Socialism is an averaging philosophy that attenuates excellence and dumbs humanity down to its lowest common denominator. It is the opposite of a meritocracy. Its philosophy is wrong because it dampens aspirations and natural ambition to progress. It celebrates the weak and vilifies the strong and striving. It does not succor soaring, achieving, innovation or creativity and therefore does not advance humanity but rather freezes its development. Socialist philosophy, for example, could discourage funding NASA and sending a person to the moon because the money could be used to provide for the needy. There would always be a socialist harping on the sidelines that it is wrong to spend money on rockets when some people are hungry. There will always be need, so socialism keeps humanity locked in a Sisyphean society forever condemned to pushing that rock up the hill of need.

## Negativity

Socialism is a negative philosophy because it divides, denies and causes dependence. It divides humanity into rich and poor, able and unable, giver and taker and taxpayer and non-taxpayer. It denies the able person's right to keep the fruits of personal labors and in doing so negates the ethic of reward for effort. Worse, it causes dependence when it provides according to need without condition. It is a philosophy that discourages incentive, attenuates effort and penalizes its most able citizens. It is not a unifying philosophy, it is a divisive one. Rather than focus on creating abundance for all it focuses on taking from some to give to others. Capitalism and free enterprise are the opposite. They are positive philosophies because they are based on merit, incentive and desert. They are philosophies that offer opportunities to all; everyone has the opportunity to get rich.

## Bluntness, Fragility, and Arrogance

The socialistic philosophy is a strange mix of these traits. It is blunt because it coercively imposes its philosophy. It is rarely a voluntary political system that naturally brings opposition. It is never universally accepted in the same way as democracy. It easily segues to extremism because it has no self-centering or self-correcting mechanisms like the competition mechanisms of democracy and capitalism. It is the wildly thrown baseball at civilization's plate glass window. Socialism is also fragile because it is a synthetic artifice that does not fit with nature; there is no socialism in nature. Nature does not redistribute wealth. Technology is only as good as the nearest light switch and socialism is only as good as the coercive power of government.

Socialism is arrogant because it defies nature. It is an attempt to arrogantly impose human will onto nature. Like many eighteenth century gardens where everything was planned, symmetrical, ordered, trimmed and box-like, socialism endeavors to impose a wayward human idea onto a reluctant nature. Socialism does not plant a natural garden like capitalism with native plants, indefinite boarders and free-flowing design, a garden that requires only occasional weeding and tending. Socialist gardens do not thrive in nature: the location is always wrong, there is never enough sun or water and the garden must be constantly trimmed and mowed. They require constant maintenance. The capitalist garden thrives in nature, and the socialist garden dies without constant human maintenance.

Socialists arrogantly usurp the right to be judge and jury for society. They presumptuously arrogate the right to determine how much the individual shall earn, how wealthy one may become and how much success one may enjoy. They arrogantly usurp the role of deciding for the individual their potential. They assume the role of dictator in order to dictate to others what they may or may not be or have. They haughtily and rapaciously grab for themselves what is ultimately the individual's natural right of choice. Socialism is an arrogant philosophy.

**Human Spirit**

On a deeper level, socialism is a philosophy that violates the human spirit. It makes people automatons and slaves. It enervates the human psyche, attenuates individual will and lessens personal freedom. It undermines free will. It makes people dependent and reliant and strips humans of their dignity. It dampens initiative and the joy of achievement and, given enough time, it takes the human spirit.

# Chapter Five

## The Vision

It is unique in the history of humanity that a group of intelligent, educated, experienced and brave souls has the opportunity to conceive what could be the best form of government. It is precious to have philosophers who carefully consider and weigh the timeless and universal ideals to which humans aspire, ideals history uses to judge the quality of any government. It is one thing to know these ideals of freedom, justice, equality, opportunity and freedom from oppression and another to make them work. America was fortunate to have such a group of such people who gave it the opportunity. These individuals were this country's Founding Fathers, and their work is embodied in the Declaration of Independence and the Constitution of the United States of America. It is as if the history of all humanity's past ideas and aspirations converged in 1776 with the formulation of the American form of government, a form of government that extends a beacon of light to all people of this planet and makes everyone want to come here to live. The highest and best form of government was what the Founding Fathers envisioned.

These Founding Fathers did not create a nation based on the principles of socialism. They did not intend to create a government that controlled the means of production or distribution of wealth or to require people work to their ability and receive according to their need. Rather, they envisioned a government that was of, for and by all the people, a republican form of democracy that guaranteed life, liberty and the pursuit of happiness. That political system contained a Bill of Rights protecting citizens from the government and the tyranny of the majority. These rights include habeas corpus, religious and political freedom, freedom of speech and assembly, freedom of the press and protection from unreasonable search and seizure. These rights also included the need for probable cause, the right not to incriminate oneself, the right to a speedy trial, protection from cruel and unusual punishment, the right to equal protection under the law and the right not to be deprived of life, liberty or property by the government without the due process of law. These timeless and universal ideals make for the highest and best form of government for citizens, and these are the ideals embodied in America's charter. These rights protect the citizen from both government and the majority's tyranny.

The original author of this charter was Thomas Jefferson. Jefferson was one of those rare individuals who appear every thousand years, a seminal individual in the history of humankind. He was both an idealist dreamer and an intellectual visionary. He was the author of the Declaration of Independence and contributor to the Constitution. He was one of America's Founding Fathers who believed in a minimalist government that pursued a *noiseless course…unattractive of notice*. His government was small, limited and invisible. He thought such a government should be frugal, live within a budget, tax very little and have low debt. He longed for a *world where government disappeared*. Jefferson's vision of government is what America was and should be. It is the highest and best form of government.

Such a government would guarantee freedom, and in particular individual freedom, or, in the true sense of the word, a freedom that grants the right to be left alone or unfettered by government and guarantees a governmental system that embodies justice. This is not a normative justice but rather a timeless and universal moral justice that applies to everyone, a justice where everyone is afforded equal opportunity and treated equally under the law; it is a justice administered by the rule of law. It is a government where taxation is fair, low, proportional and levied only to support essential governmental services. These functions would include defense, peacekeeping, preventing and protecting individuals from force and fraud, maintaining a system of administering justice and providing for certain essential governmental services. It would have a tax system that tolerates the unequal distribution of wealth and gives the individual the freedom to accumulate property.

It would be a form of government that would engender strong social norms, morality integrity, virtue, a society of citizens who are personally responsible and accountable for their actions and a society of self-reliant, prudential independent individualists. It should be a meritocracy where industry is succored and effort is rewarded. Such a society would encourage free enterprise and capitalism. Such a society would naturally be optimistic, bright, happy, gregarious and enterprising, and such a society would naturally have wealth and abundance. It would be a society that embraces many of the ideals of libertarianism without the anarchy. The citizens of such a society would have compassion for their fellow citizens, but all assistance would be voluntary, short term and designed to teach others to fish — a form of assistance that teaches people how to help themselves and encourages them to be self-reliant.

It would be a constitutional and liberal (in the nineteenth century European meaning of the word) kind of government. It would be a form of government where the coercive powers of the state are limited and the majority's ability to wield arbitrary, capricious and authoritarian power over the minority is restricted. It would not be an unfettered form of democracy but rather a liberal one that requires the majority to observe certain principles including the inalienable rights of personal and individual freedom and justice. It would be a form of government that gives all citizens the freedom to decide for themselves just how much they wish to participate in the collective group.

Many, no doubt, will consider this vision unrealistic because things have changed. Why would they say this? This is the vision upon which America was founded and for which it worked for over a hundred years. This vision is the reason America became great and the reason everyone wants to come here. This is not an unrealistic vision, it is one that did and does work. Some may say America changed because it had to respond to certain issues such as social unrest. However, if the theme of this book is correct, it may very well be that the socialistic changes that have occurred are themselves the source of any future unrest. They are the unrealistic changes to what was a wonderful ideal that may eventually bring about the downfall of this beloved America. Nothing has changed; the ideals and reasons for the inception of America's original form of government remain. They will never go away. If there has been any change, it is that socialism has taken its death grip hold on this country and is slowly strangling the life out of America's beautifully conceived form of government.

In the introduction I wrote that his book is written to those who are wavering in the belief of the American dream. That dream is the vision that has just been described. You may be disenchanted with capitalist America but compare its benefits with those of socialistic countries described throughout this book. You have unprecedented freedom; you live in a vital, peaceful and wealthy country; you probably have a job; you are usually treated justly; and you have vast opportunity. You are the envy of many people throughout the world who dearly wish they could come and live here. These are benefits that have been gained under the American vision and not socialism. If you remain disenchanted with the American dream let me ask you, which socialist country would you rather emigrate to? Russia, Cuba, Venezuela, North Korea or perhaps China, and what is your answer? The truth is America is one of the best places in the world to live, and it was the American vision that helped make it that way. I believe that your best possible life is in America without the plague.

Rome's greatest politician, Cicero, once wrote that the key to greatness is to bring the different classes together and resolve their differences. In truth, Americans have more in common than not. It is in everyone's interests to have freedom, justice, freedom from oppression, freedom from arbitrary and capricious authority, wealth, basic services, opportunity and strong social norms. It is not in everyone's interests for some to have artificial advantages, privilege, poverty, dependence, tyranny, immorality and a sick economy. The Founding Fathers' vision is a philosophy that is in the common interests of all Americans. It is a vision that brings all Americans together, and it is a vision all Americans should strive to achieve.

# Conclusion

Alexis de Tocqueville came to America in 1831 and published his book *Democracy in America* in 1835. In that book, he predicted there was *a species of oppression…which democratic nations are menaced…unlike anything which ever before existed in the world.* He said it was a new and indefinable oppression. It was an oppression that stands *above this race of men… [an] immense and tutelary power, which takes upon itself alone to secure their gratifications, and to watch over their fate.* It was despotism of a different character never before seen among people, despotism that *would be more extensive and more mild; it would degrade men without tormenting them.* This new power would take *each member of the community in its powerful grasp, and [fashion] him at will.* With this power, it would cause *a network of small complicated rules, minute and uniform* that would soften, bend, and guide people. It would be a force that

> compresses, enervates, extinguishes, and
> stupefies a people, till each…is reduced

to be nothing better than a flock of timid and industrious animals, of which the government is the shepherd. It would be an all-powerful form of government...[that combines] the principle of centralization and that of popular sovereignty.

Tocqueville published these words four years before the word socialism appeared in the English language, eight years before Karl Marx published the *Communist Manifesto*, thirty-seven years before Marx's socialist organization First International moved to New York, and fifty-three years before Bernard Shaw wrote in his *Fabian Essays* that *the economic side of the democratic ideal is, in fact, socialism itself.* Tocqueville could not define this form of despotism because it had not yet been developed, or even named. The despotism in democracies he was describing is socialism.

The plague is in America today, it is becoming despotic and it will ruin this country. It is a terrible process. The philosophy is legalizing theft with its policies of wealth redistribution and progressive taxation. It is a philosophy that is slowly enervating America's strong by taking their incentive on one hand and creating a vast dependent class on the other. The philosophy is cannibalizing America's most able and productive citizens. This utilitarian philosophy is not grounded, which is perpetrating injustice and causing the gradual decay of America's moral base. The philosophy is taking Americans' freedom and individuality and is eating away at America's wealth like a parasite slowing consuming its host. This furtive philosophy depends on citizens' ignorance of its means and consequences to advance. It is a totalitarian, tyrannical and despotic philosophy that is bastardizing America's origins and reason for being. The socialist philosophy's time has passed because its promises come at too high a price. Its promises are security and equality, but its price is freedom and justice. This unrealistic philosophy has leveled other cultures and is now pulling down America's.

Something is going terribly wrong with America; the country appears to be sliding into a cultural war brought upon by socialism. What the Germans call *kultur* is beginning to decay and the American spirit, its ethos, is weakening. Its citizens are losing their bearings and vigor. The ideals of liberty, justice for all and political equality are waning. It is happening, and the world's longest surviving democracy, like the age of Pericles in ancient Athens two thousand years ago, may soon exist only in the history books.

# Sources

Following are some abbreviated sources used for *The Plague*. The sources for all quotes used in this book can be found in the endnotes of my book Socialism in America.

*A Study of History*, Arnold J. Toynbee

*America: A Narrative History*, George Brown Tindall and David Emory Shi

*American Labor*, Henry Pelling

*America's Maligned and Misunderstood Trade Deficit*, Daniel T. Griswold

*An Intellectual History of Liberalism*, Charles Murray

*Andrè Gide*, G.W. Ireland

*Argentine crisis lingers, forcing many into poverty*, Larry Rohter

*Black's Law Dictionary*, Sixth Edition, Bryan A. Garner

*Cicero*, Anthony Everitt

*Democracy in America*, Alexis de Tocqueville

*Design for Utopia: Selected Writings of Charles Fourier*, Charles Fourier

*Dictionary of Philosophy and Religion: Eastern and Western Thought*, William L. Reese,

*Domestic Tranquility: A Brief Against Feminism*, Carolyn F. Gragulia

*Eat the Rich*, P. J. O'Rourke,

*Economics*, Paul A. Samuelson

Email from the French Embassy in America to this author dated December 17, 2003

*Emerson: The Mind on Fire*, Robert D. Richardson, Jr.

*Essential Works of Lenin*, Henry M. Christman

*Fifty Key Thinkers on History*, Marnie Hughes-Warrington

*Founding Brothers: The Revolutionary Generation*, Joseph J. Ellis

*Frozen Desire: The Meaning of Money*, James Buchan

Gender gap widens, *USA Today*

Getting before and after-school care, *USA Today*

*Grandfather Economic Report*, Michael Hodges

*History of Socialism*, Harry W. Laidler

How federal government gets and spends money, *USA Today*

*Intellectuals*, Paul Johnson

*Let Us Talk of Many Things: the Collected Speeches*, William F. Buckley

*Masterpieces of World Philosophy*, Frank N. Magill

*Men are from Mars, Women are from Venus*, John Gray

*Modern Biology*, Truman J. Moon, Paul B. Mann and James H. Otto

News Hour Report: Balanced Budget Amendment and Fiscal Responsibility, MacNeil/Lehrer Productions

*Of the Social Contract, or Principles of Political Right*, Jean-Jacques Rousseau

*On Liberty*, John Stuart Mill

*One Nation, Two Cultures*, Gertrude Himmelfarb

*People of the Lie*, Scott M. Peck

*Political Science*, Robert A. Heineman

*Politics*, Kenneth Minogue

*Slander*, Ann Coulter

*Social Organization, the Science of Man and other Writings*, Henri de Saint-Simon

*Socialism: Utopian and Scientific*, Friederich Engels

*Stalin*, Edvard Radzinsky

*Taxation and Justice*, Edward W. Younkins

The 2000 Democratic National Platform: Prosperity, Progress and Peace, www.democrats.org

*The American Sphinx*, Joseph J. Ellis

*The American Tradition in Literature*, Bradley Scully, Richmond Croom Beatty and E. Hudson Long,

*The Anarchists*, James Joll

*The Biographical Encyclopedia of Philosophy*, Henry Thomas

*The Constitution of Liberty*, Friedrich Hayek

*The Failure of U. S. Tax Policy*, Sheldon D. Pollack

*The French Socialist Experiment*, John S.Ambler

*The House of Morgan*, Ron Chernow

*The Philosophy of Law*, Fredrick Schauer and Walter Sinnott-Armstrong

*The Road to Serfdom*, F. A. Hayek

'Til politics do us part, *USA Today*

*The Worldly Philosophers*, Robert L. Heilbroner

*Toward a Democratic Left*, Michael Harrington

*Wealth & Democracy*, Kevin Phillips

# About the Author

John Bowman lives in Portland, Oregon, where he raised three daughters with his wife, Kathy. He is the author of numerous books on philosophy, real estate, politics, sports, words, Stoicism and humor. He received a Bachelor of Arts degree in 1973 from Whitman College, a Bachelor of Arts degree in philosophy in 1993 from Portland State University and a Master of Interdisciplinary Studies degree in philosophy and history in 2010 from Oregon State University. His master's thesis, titled *Stoicism, Enkrasia and Happiness*, surveyed the ancient philosophy of stoicism and particularly the famous Roman stoic Seneca. A complete list of his books follows.

The author welcomes reader comments, observations and rebuttals. His books and biography can be viewed on his website at www.johnlbowman.com, or he can be reached by e-mail at author@johnlbowman.com.

Thanks for reading my book, I hope you liked it.

# Other Books by John L. Bowman

*Reflections on Man and the Human Condition*
*Selected Topics in Philosophy*
*Nobody's Perfect*
*How to Succeed in Commercial Real Estate*
*Socialism in America*
*God's Lecture*
*A Reader's Companion*
*Stoicism, Enkrasia and Happiness*
*Aegean Summer*
*The Art of Volleyball Hitting*
*Graduate School*
*Provocative and Contemplative Quotations*
*On Law*
*A Reference Guide to Stoicism*
*A Reader's Companion II*
*Democracy and Why It Will Fail in America*
*Philosophy and Happiness*
*My Travels (unpublished)*
*How to Get Rich*
*A Reader's Companion III*
*I Knew this Would Happen*
*On Humans*
*I Knew this Would Happen*
*Tupac*